"Nico."

She sounded breathless, as if she'd been running.

"Good morning, Beth. I've come to offer you the family's condolences on the loss of your husband, and to talk about some inheritance issues."

Her eyes slid to the windowpane in the door, then back to him. "Surely any paperwork can be handled by attorneys? You didn't need to travel all this way."

"Oh, but I did. I'm here only for the weekend, so we'll talk today, in one hour. At my hotel room."

Despite his best efforts, he'd never managed to control his craving for the woman who betrayed him. He'd volunteered to finalize the paperwork in person regarding his dead brother's share of the family vineyards because he had to see Beth one more time.

To have her in his bed one more time.

Dear Reader,

There's something about a tortured hero, something I find irresistible. And my heroine, Beth, finds Nico Jordan quite irresistible, too—so I knew she'd need a very good reason to have left him seven years ago (though he wasn't tortured back then, just the plain old garden-variety irresistible!). Luckily Nico finds Beth just as tempting.

As for their setting…a couple of years ago I visited the Marlborough region of New Zealand, famous for its vineyards and wineries. With its landscape of endless rows of vines and its huge supply of wine-tasting rooms, it's such a romantic location—the perfect backdrop for Nico and Beth's struggle to come back together.

I spent quite a bit of time tasting wine…er, researching… for this story, so I hope you enjoy reading Nico and Beth's story as much as I enjoyed writing it!

Best wishes,

Rachel

RACHEL BAILEY

THE BLACKMAILED BRIDE'S SECRET CHILD

Silhouette® Desire

Published by Silhouette Books

America's Publisher of Contemporary Romance

SILHOUETTE BOOKS

PLEASE RECYCLE · THIS PRODUCT IS RECYCLABLE

ISBN-13: 978-0-373-73011-7

Recycling programs
for this product may
not exist in your area.

THE BLACKMAILED BRIDE'S SECRET CHILD

Visit Silhouette Books at www.eHarlequin.com

Printed in U.S.A.

Books by Rachel Bailey

Silhouette Desire

Claiming His Bought Bride #1992
The Blackmailed Bride's Secret Child #1998

RACHEL BAILEY

developed a serious book addiction at a young age (via Peter Rabbit and Jemima Puddleduck) and has never recovered. Just how she likes it. She went on to gain degrees in psychology and social work, but is now living her dream—writing romance for a living.

She lives on a piece of paradise on Australia's Sunshine Coast with her hero and four dogs, and loves to sit with a dog or two, overlooking the trees and reading books from her ever-growing to-be-read pile.

Rachel would love to hear from you and can be contacted through her Web site, www.rachelbailey.com.

To my mother, Noela.
For her support and indefatigable belief in me.

Thanks to

Diana Ventimiglia and Jennifer Schober
for their wisdom and guidance.

Barbara Jeffcott Geris
and her gorgeous husband, George,
for the wine information (though any mistakes are mine).

Lisa, Robbie, Sharon and Barb
for their encouragement and brilliance.

One

Nico Jordan surveyed the front of the ranch-style house where his half brother's widow lived, and scowled into the frosty morning air. She'd left *him* for Kent and this pretentious piece of real estate?

Well, to be fair, Kent's personal fortune had probably bought Beth several houses besides this one, and jewels by the bucket—things Nico wouldn't have been able to afford back when he was twenty-four.

Things had changed in the last five years.

More things than he cared to remember.

But Kent was dead, Beth was now a widow and Nico had a job to do. He rolled up the pages in his hand and knocked on the door with a clenched fist. He'd volunteered to finalize the paperwork in person regarding his dead brother's share of the family vineyards because he had to see Beth one more time. To have her in his bed one more time.

Despite his best efforts, he'd never managed to control his craving for the woman who'd betrayed him.

He lifted his fist to knock again but the door opened with a whoosh of warm air and then Beth stood there, more beautiful than he remembered, her so-familiar Cupid's bow mouth open, her sapphire blue eyes wide.

Suddenly he was transported back five years to the last time they'd made love among the pinot noir vines on his family's estate in Australia. They'd both pledged undying love that day—the day before she'd left the country to marry his brother.

"Nico." She sounded breathless, as if she'd been running, but there was no flush on her cheeks. In fact, she looked pale.

Her strawberry blond hair was shorter, in a pixie cut now, which only made her heart-shaped face sweeter. His gaze swept down—she'd lost some weight, leaving her a little too thin, but that didn't stop the pull of dark desire that flooded his system.

Yet he offered her no more than a cynical smile. "Good morning, Beth. I've come to offer you the family's condolences on the loss of your husband, and to talk about some inheritance issues."

Beth's eyes darted to the side and she turned, hurriedly scanning the lavish room. He could see through to a living room beyond—also decorated in tasteful elegance. Then she stepped out onto the porch, closing the door firmly, but quietly behind her. "Thank you for the condolences. That was thoughtful of…your family."

There was no love lost between his family and Beth—his father blamed her in part for Kent moving here to New Zealand to manage these minor vineyards and cutting most family ties. *That* wasn't the crime Nico held her accountable for, however. "No trouble at all for the widow of our dear Kent."

She had the grace to look unsettled. Though she should feel worse than merely "unsettled" after the anguish she'd caused him.

Her eyes slid to the windowpane in the door then back to him. "Surely any paperwork can be handled by attorneys? You didn't need to come all the way from Australia."

He leaned one arm on the closed door, dipping his head several inches closer. "Oh, *bella,* but I did."

She flinched at the use of the endearment, the one he'd whispered so often on lazy afternoons in her parents' hammock, or in the heat of passion when she lay under him.

"If we have to talk, then not here. I'll meet you somewhere." Her voice betrayed nerves—and determination.

"Are you telling me I'm not welcome in my own brother's house?" He didn't bother to hide the irony in his tone—he knew his brother would have stabbed him in the back rather than invite him into his home. Their lifelong, bitter rivalry had reached its peak after Kent's marriage to Beth. She had been immediately whisked overseas to sever all ties with her past, but even worse, to maintain the estrangement, Kent's son had never seen his grandfather or his Uncle Nico. A situation Nico intended to rectify.

He ran his gaze over Beth again. Kent had probably been wise to be paranoid about his wife. Had Beth strayed across Nico's path after her marriage, he wouldn't have thought twice about poaching on his brother's territory. Kent hadn't bothered with those rules.

But Kent was gone.

Beth darted another look inside and raised a hand to circle her throat. "Nico, do this for me. If we have to talk, meet me another day, somewhere else."

What was she hiding? Was she continuing Kent's plan to keep his son from his family? Or did she have a lover stashed away? Perhaps both.

"Five minutes alone and you're already asking favors, *bella*." Nico let his hand fall from the door, considering his options. Despite his determination to harden his heart, the plea in her eyes tugged at him, made it almost impossible to refuse her anything. But he must remember she was a good actress. This was the woman who'd strung him along for eleven months and then left him as soon as she got a better offer from his richer half brother.

And yet…

Deciding to grant this one favor, Nico blew out a breath. "I'm here only for the weekend, so we'll talk today, in one hour. At my hotel room."

"In one hour?" She reached behind and grasped the door to support herself. "That will be difficult. Perhaps tomorrow?"

He'd conceded enough. He turned to go. "If you're not there in one hour, I'll be back. I'll also make a petition to the court that your son has access to his grandfather. The papers are drawn up and in the car ready to be lodged."

He and this small boy were the only family his father had left, which was tragic for a family man like Tim Jordan. Nico had always been exceptionally close to his father and he'd do whatever it took to bring some joy to the older man, especially now he was so ill.

"Nico, you don't understand—"

Her voice, fraught with panic, didn't move him. He had no time to listen to her excuses.

"One hour, Beth. I'm staying at The Imperial." He strode toward his car, not looking back.

One hour later, Beth stood outside Nico's penthouse suite, barely able to get her fuddled brain to think clearly.

Nico, the only man she'd ever loved, was back. The man she'd protected by sacrificing her own hopes for happiness.

As soon as his car had left her drive, she'd run to find her son and taken him to her parents' house nearby. Kent had bought the place for them, not out of the goodness of his heart, but to ensure she had no reason to visit Australia again. They were already set to have him for the night and following day, allowing her to attend the launch of Kent's final white wine blend this evening. They'd been thrilled to have the extra morning with little Marco—or Mark, as Kent had christened him.

Only she called her four-year-old son by the name she used in her heart.

Her parents must have guessed her baby's true parentage, though——her reddish blond hair and fair skin mixed with Kent's ruddy complexion could never have made a child with strong Mediterranean coloring. Marco's olive skin, chocolate eyes and dark hair were so obviously the coloring Nico had inherited from his own mother. However Beth's parents had never said a word and she'd silently thanked them for that.

But if Nico saw him…

No. Not yet. Beth wrapped her arms around her waist. She couldn't let him near his own son until it was safe. The consequences for Nico were still too great to tell him. She just needed to keep the secret while he was here on this trip. It wouldn't be long before she could come clean about everything.

In the meantime, convenient or not, if Nico wanted to see her today, then she'd go along with it. She knew what the stakes were—he didn't.

With a heavy heart, she rapped on the door.

She heard footfalls across tiles, then the door dragged open.

He stood there, tall and broad and darkly beautiful, and her pulse raced into overdrive without him doing a single thing. His face gave her no indication of his thoughts, no encouragement, but she needed none. The mere sight of him made her a little dizzy with joy, just as it had an hour ago. As it always had when they were younger.

"Give me your coat." He held out a strong bronze hand.

Beth untied the belt of her long black coat and let it fall to her wrists. He took the garment and hung it from a hook on the wall, then heat flared in his dark eyes as he surveyed her thoroughly. Finally, he smiled in satisfaction and his gaze rested on hers.

She glanced down at her loose, ankle-length, woolen pink dress. Her clothes were all similar—none were fitted, none accentuated her as a woman. For five years, she'd avoided calling sexual attention to herself. For five years...ever since she'd lost Nico.

Although, the hunger in his glittering eyes now seemed to make a mockery of her efforts to disguise herself.

He opened the door wider and let her through.

As she walked across the opulent room to the window, the hair at the back of her neck stood on end and she knew he'd watched her progress. She'd always known when Nico was looking at her. She turned slowly from the bird's eye view of the wintry vineyards to find him blatantly staring. Her skin tightened and her breasts begged for his skilled touch—but too much was at stake to be swayed by her body's physical responses. Nico could lose his inheritance, his career, even his identity.

He held up a bottle of champagne. "Drink?"

Now of all times, she needed a clear head. "No, thank you."

He poured something from the bar for himself. If his tastes hadn't changed, it'd be a pinot noir.

While he was distracted with his task, she drank in the sight of him—the thick, dark hair she'd once slid her fingers through; face a little too long to be symmetrical, but still more dear to her than anything...except the same face in miniature. Their precious son.

Oh, God, she couldn't stand this tension one minute longer—she had to know. "Tell me what you came to New Zealand to say, Nico." Being able to say his name again gave her heart wings, but she wouldn't let herself forget what she risked by being here.

Seemingly relaxed, he leaned a hip on the galley-kitchen counter. "I want several things, but let's start with my nephew."

Her heart stalled and she felt the blood drain from her head. "You want Mark?"

Nico looked down his proud nose, appearing every inch the Italian aristocrat that his mother had been. "He's of my blood and he's lost his father. I'd like to build a relationship with the boy."

For a crazy moment, she'd thought he wanted to take her son away. But—she swallowed—this was almost as bad. "You know that's not what Kent would have wanted. You two had sworn to never set eyes on the other again."

It'd been the breach that sent Nico off on his own for three years—making his own millions on the stock market, becoming a tabloid darling as one of Australia's richest playboys. She'd tormented herself by reading the magazines, insanely jealous of any woman photographed on his arm, yet praying he was happy.

"What Kent wanted is irrelevant at this point. Do you

think he wanted to die and leave his son fatherless?" He waved away her protest. "I will see the child and I will become an uncle to him."

As much as Nico may believe that, if she allowed the contact, the truth would come to light too soon, and he wouldn't thank her for the consequences. He would more likely resent her, possibly blame her.

"He might be fatherless, but he has his mother. Decisions about who my son will know, and when, are mine. He's happy with his life here and he's close to his grandparents and friends." She bit the inside of her cheek hard, knowing she had to be cruel to be kind, but still hating saying the words. "He doesn't need you."

Nico took a deliberate sip of his drink then rested his glass on the bench he still leaned on. "Regardless of whether he needs me or not, he has a heritage. His family has been in the wine industry for generations, it's in our blood, in our DNA. Mark will inherit his share of that business one day and he needs to grow to understand it."

It's in our blood, in our DNA.

Beth flinched. Nico believed it was in his blood.

How often had she heard him talk of his heritage this way when they were together? It would destroy him to know the information detailed in letters Kent had obtained, that Nico was an illegitimate son—not a son at all. The vineyard was no more in his blood than it was in hers.

And it would crush him to find he had no biological connection to the father he loved. She'd always thought Nico and Tim seemed more like brothers as they worked together on their estate. Their love and admiration for each other was beautiful to see.

When Kent had ambushed her with the letters—using them to blackmail her into marriage—she'd known she had no choice. Tim Jordan had suffered three major heart attacks only eight months earlier and the whole family had been cautioned by the medical staff that he needed to avoid stress.

If she'd refused to comply, Kent would have released the pages, maybe even splashed them through the tabloids. Nico would have been destroyed and Tim's stress at finding out Nico wasn't his son could have brought on another heart attack. She'd known Kent didn't care about jeopardizing his own father's life—he was still bitter that Tim had divorced his mother for Nico's more than twenty years earlier.

Kent had never forgiven any of those involved—Nico and Nico's mother, or their father—for the marriage that had usurped him and his mother, Minnie. The marriage that had seen them moved from the main house to a cottage next door.

It had been up to Beth to stop Kent the only way she could—by agreeing to his proposal.

That very day, she'd left the country without a word to the man she loved like no other. The man standing before her.

But everything was different now. Kent was dead. She hadn't yet found where he'd hidden the letters, but that was only a matter of time.

From this point on, decisions were hers alone.

After an agonizing amount of thought, Beth had

decided to come clean and tell Nico everything…but not until after Tim passed away. According to medical opinion, that would likely be in the next twelve months. Severe stress might tragically shorten that time period and that was a chance she couldn't take.

She walked to the windows, needing a greater distance between them for this conversation. "Mark will be fine. He spent time with Kent on the vineyards here and in the cellar." Though, in truth, that time had been rare.

Nico straightened, eyes determined. "But who will continue that education now? You have an obligation to your son to let him know his family. It's his birthright to learn from a Jordan about our legacy."

She rubbed her upper arms, chilled to the bone by the truth in his words. Marco did deserve time with his *real* father. Tearing her gaze from Nico's, she turned to look at the view of the naked vines waiting in limbo for spring before they could burst forth with life again. She'd been in that same limbo for five years.

She felt him move behind her. "But let's not fight, *bella*." His voice was deeper, seductive.

His searing hands rested on her almost bare shoulders and smoothed a path to her upper arms and back again. The touch ignited sensations in her body that she hadn't felt since he had last lain his hands on her skin. Five long years. His palms trailed down to her wrists and he moved a step closer so she could feel his body heat from behind.

She'd dreamed so often of this moment, of being here with him again…but this was wrong—nothing like her fantasies at all. This wasn't the sweet, tender Nico of years ago.

Though why would he be? As far as he was concerned, she'd betrayed him. And he was right—no matter how pure her motives, she *had* betrayed him. Even acknowledging that, it hurt to know he no longer loved or trusted her.

She stepped away from his touch and faced him. "What are you doing, Nico? You can't turn up out of the blue and assume rights that ended when we broke up."

"When *we* broke up." He reached out and gently took her hands in his. "I'm not sure *we* is the right word when talking about the end of our relationship." His alluring tone belied the meaning of his words, but his eyes didn't lie. They were pained, tormented.

Her knees weakened, seeing the hurt she'd caused him, so she locked them to stop from swaying and firmed her resolve. "This is not the best time to get into that. You said you had paperwork to discuss."

"You have a good point," he said, voice dark. He ran his thumbs in circles on her palms, setting off a domino effect of sparks throughout her body. "When will be an appropriate time to discuss our relationship, do you think?"

With great effort, she wrenched her hands away and tucked them under her crossed arms. "I have no interest in the topic at all. I consider it closed."

Eyebrow raised, he stepped back to retrieve his wineglass. "I beg to differ."

"It takes two to have a conversation."

He sank down into an armchair and sipped his wine. "It takes two for many things. Conversations. Relationships. Love."

She raised her chin a little. "I said I won't discuss this."

Nico shrugged, but there was a gleam in his eye. "Then we're at an impasse. Take a seat."

Warily—Nico didn't normally give up once he'd decided he wanted something—she sat in the farthest chair from him, a dining stool near the kitchenette.

"There are papers that you need to sign as Mark's guardian. I don't know what Kent arranged for the personal fortune his mother gave him, but you probably know he didn't yet own any stocks in the family business."

"Yes," she said, nodding once. "Your father still owns them." Kent had never shared much about his financial status beyond the allowance he gave her to run the household, but the lawyer acting as Kent's executor had explained this much.

"The shares in Jordan Wines were to be divided equally between us, his two sons, in four years' time or on his death, whichever came first. The three of us had already signed a Deed of Gift to that effect." He picked up a sheaf of papers from the coffee table. "Now he wants Kent's share to go to Mark and he doesn't want to wait. He's been deeply affected by Kent's death," he said, his gaze fierce, "especially as they'd been in a semi-estrangement that he still doesn't understand."

Beth swallowed. They both knew her marriage had been the start of those tensions. But she'd never wanted this—any of it. In fact, they were the two people she'd been trying to protect—Nico and his father. If Nico knew the truth, he'd be put in the untenable position of choosing between two evils: his strong sense of right and wrong would compel him to tell his father the truth, which could lead to him being disinherited, and bringing on another heart attack, endangering his father's life. To say nothing of his father being haunted in his final days, knowing his dearest son wasn't even his.

Or, Nico could choose to keep the truth from his father and the secrecy would eat at him like acid. His relationship with Tim would never be as close, as solid, ever again. Damned if he did and damned if he didn't. Beth *couldn't* put Nico in that situation.

He swirled the deep red liquid in his glass. "Dad wants to divide the company between Mark and me in the next few months."

Beth felt her jaw slacken. "But Mark is a little boy!"

He shook his head dismissively. "No one expects a three-year old to inherit this kind of fortune right now."

Kent had told his whole family that Mark was born a year later than he had been—not wanting Nico to put two and two together. And since none of the family in Australia had ever met her son, it'd been a relatively easy charade to pull off. She wouldn't comment on that particular problem yet— she'd find a way to fix this.

She spread damp hands over the pink fabric on her lap. "I think it would be better for Mark if your father leaves all this for now. It's too much weight on small shoulders, even to just know it's coming."

"We agree at least on that. But it's my father's money and his decision to make. He's naming you and me as joint trustees for Mark's share until he's twenty-one."

Suddenly, Beth couldn't breathe. Joint trustees? After Kent's death, she'd started to rebuild the pieces of her life. Had made a plan to expose all the secrets once Tim passed away. Then Nico had knocked on her door and scattered all her plans—and her thinking—just by his presence.

And now this. It was too much, too soon. She labored to draw in enough air but still couldn't fill her lungs.

Nico's expression changed almost imperceptibly from arrogance to guarded concern. "Beth? Are you all right?"

She needed air, fresh air, and to be away from the man of both her dreams and her nightmares. She dashed for the door, picked up her bag and coat and ran as fast as she could.

Two

Nico gave her twenty minutes head start before jumping into his rented Alfa Romeo, gunning the engine, and following.

Twenty wasted minutes where he'd thought she was genuinely upset. His first impulse had been to follow her, make sure she was okay, but he'd tamped that down, knowing he was the last person she'd want to see. Given their estrangement and current situation, he'd only distress her more.

Then he'd remembered what a consummate actress she was.

Any woman who could make him believe she was in love with him—and he'd believed it to the bottom of his soul for almost a year—was a world-class performer.

He thumped the heel of his hand on the steering wheel

as he sped past fields of bare grapevines. He couldn't believe he'd been taken in again, and so quickly!

Hot air blasted from the heater; already boiling from the inside, he jabbed the off button. Her show of distress had called to a fiercely protective streak—one he thought had died five years ago—and he'd let her walk out. But from now on he wouldn't let his guard down even an inch. He was here to meet his nephew, find Kent's copy of the Deed of Gift…and lure the woman who haunted his dreams back into his bed. For one night.

The torment of Beth's betrayal had never left—through each successful venture, each new woman that came and went within days or weeks, the pain of losing the woman he'd loved had buried itself deeper inside his chest, festering. And the occasional news through the family grapevine—such as the birth of her son to his brother—had ensured the humiliation, the *pain,* never healed.

Nico ground his teeth as he held the steering wheel in a death grip. He knew it'd been slowly killing him—so it was essential he purge it all now. He needed to make love to her one last time.

He roared into her tree-lined driveway deep in the winery's estate, and cut the engine.

Striding to the entry, he reined in his emotions. The key to success was to stay on top of his game. No outbursts from his hair-trigger temper.

He thumped on the door. "Beth, let me in."

Noises came from inside the house but none from the other side of the door. More noises, more movement—she was home, just not letting him in.

He thumped on the heavy wooden door again. "Beth, I'm not going away."

The door wrenched open to reveal Beth barefoot, in the same shapeless pink dress. Though it was shapeless, it nevertheless showed enough of her figure to fire his passion, as it'd done at his hotel room door.

She seemed troubled, but not surprised, to see him. "Nico, please leave me alone. The papers can be dealt with by our lawyers."

Not a chance. He strode past her into the warmth of her house.

Turning, he took in the room with its roaring fireplace, decorated in colors that were pure Beth—delicate pinks, pale greens and ivory. Either Kent had trusted her sense of style, or he hadn't cared.

His gaze rested on the woman who'd closed the door, but still gripped the handle behind her, as if for support.

The want, the *need* for her that always lurked below the surface surged up to flood his system. "I can't leave you alone, even if I wanted to."

"W-why?"

She'd seen it in his eyes, he knew she had—the unadulterated lust he felt had made her stammer. He took a step toward her, slowly, softly. "Because we have unfinished business."

She didn't pretend to misunderstand. "Nico, people break up all the time. Don't you think you're being a little dramatic?"

"Here's the thing, *bella*. I don't remember us breaking up. I remember making love to you in the vineyards under the light of a full moon." He took another step forward. "I remember you pledging yourself to me for eternity, and I remember driving you home."

"Nico, please—"

He held up his hand to stop her, then he snapped his fingers in her line of vision. "The next thing I know, you've left the country to marry my brother."

Her face twisted in an impersonation of guilt. "I wish I could have talked to you—"

"I can see why you didn't, though. Wouldn't want any messy situations with Nico." He planted his hands on his hips, the agony and shame of that day still raw in his chest. "Wouldn't want him to ask for an explanation or, God forbid, plead with you not to leave."

And the disgrace of it was, he *would* have pleaded. At least he'd been spared the indignity of baring his weakness. Now he would not be weak.

"Nico, I—"

"One thing I wondered, though—" he prowled another step closer, eyes narrowed "—was it a spontaneous decision when a better offer came up? Or were you using me all along to get to the richer brother?"

Like a switch had been flicked, her eyes became arctic. "Which did you decide I'd done?"

"Kent told me that he offered you money to marry him, so I'm thinking it was probably a combination of the two." And hadn't Kent been gleeful in delivering that news? In delivering the final checkmate in their lifelong rivalry. "You must have thought all your Christmases had come at once when your target offered you money to do something you'd been planning anyway." He laughed but it sounded bitter even to his own ears.

The color drained from her face—a reaction she couldn't have faked, so he'd obviously hit the nail on the head. Pain ripped through him—*more* pain, when he'd thought he'd felt all the agony he could. He pushed it away so he could continue and took a step forward. "He bought you fair and square. So tell me, Beth, what will it cost *me* to get you into my bed? I expect the price has gone up since then."

She pressed her hands to her chest. "Nico, don't do this, please."

He raised a sardonic eyebrow and closed the last distance between them, leaving their bodies almost touching. "Is it purely a cash transaction, or do you prefer real estate and jewels?"

She slid sideways, moving across the room to put a couch between them as a teardrop fell and traced a path down her cheek. "Nico, I'm sorry."

He swallowed, making himself remember that crying was an easy feat for an actress.

A second tear followed the path of the first. "You'll never know how sorry I am for what you went through."

He watched her hands turn white as they clasped together. So, perhaps she had a conscience about betraying him after all? But words came easily, and these did nothing to assuage the ache in his chest.

He took off his suit coat and threw it over the couch she was hiding behind. "You're sorry." He shook his head slowly. "You finally said it. For all it's worth."

Beth heard the dismissal in his tone and bit down on her lip. She'd once known Nico as well as she'd known herself—but *this* man was a stranger. "Will you accept my apology?"

Nico walked through an archway into her living room and paced before coming to lean a shoulder in the doorway to the hall leading to Marco's room. Thank God her son was gone for the weekend.

Nico crossed one polished black shoe over the other. "You wounded my pride by leaving with my brother. That's not an easy thing to forgive."

"I understand that." She softened her voice. "Honestly, I do."

He pushed off the doorway to stand tall and proud. "Do you really? You're sorry for humiliating me in front of my family? For selling yourself to a man who hated me from the day I was born?"

She knew the real hurt that he wouldn't voice. *For breaking his heart.*

If *her* heart hadn't stopped bleeding since being wrenched from its home with his, how much worse must it have been for him to be left behind?

Then, as if a veil lifted from before her eyes, she glimpsed deep inside him to the real Nico, so loving and sweet beneath the hard man. The Nico he hid from everyone, even himself.

Before she could change her mind, she went to him, but she didn't do it for the bitter man before her. She did it for the Nico she'd loved more than life itself—for the pain she'd unwillingly caused. She did it for the Nico who was still somewhere inside him, hurting.

An arm's length away, heart racing, she stopped.

He watched her closely, face inscrutable.

Being this close to him made her ache to move the last step. To touch him. To taste his skin. To feel his touch. Her body reacted to him as if no time had passed. As if they still belonged to each other.

But that time of belonging was long gone. And she was more sorry for that than he could ever know.

She held out her hand, a peace offering, trying to convey the regret that overwhelmed her without using words, which he now distrusted.

Heat flared in his brooding eyes and his jaw clenched, but he didn't move.

He felt it, too.

The explosive sparks they generated when they were together. It'd been there again since he'd knocked on her door earlier this morning. Perhaps what she was doing would set a match to the tinder, but she remained standing, arm outstretched, offering him her hand.

Then his gaze softened and he came to her, wrapping her in his embrace and pressing her close. His body felt different to her memories—more solid, he'd filled out beautifully. She felt him shudder as she wound her arms around his neck, and they stood there, motionless for timeless minutes.

But then she pulled away, not meeting his eyes.

He didn't make a move to stop her.

She turned and walked away, needing space from the waves of emotion and desire still rolling through her.

"Beth," he rasped, but she couldn't turn back or she knew she'd take him to her bed and that would only make everything so much more difficult…make his leaving utterly unbearable.

She'd always worn her heart on her sleeve with him, and if she was to keep the secret from him about his illegitimacy until after his father passed away, then she *must* keep emotional distance.

She'd apologized, and that was the last time she could afford to drop her guard around him.

If he caught her in a moment of vulnerability, and asked her the right question—could she be sure she wouldn't blurt out the secret that could hurt him and his father so deeply? She'd been incredibly fond of Tim Jordan, and for him to lose the son of his heart while he was terribly sick would be cruelty. The only solution that was fair to Tim and Nico was to wait.

The phone rang in the next room and she had to restrain herself from running to the kitchen for the salvation of the call.

"Hello?"

"Mrs. Jordan, it's Noela from the winery."

Kent's secretary. As Beth leaned back against the bench, she caught sight of Nico from the corner of her eye. He stood in the doorway, leaning a hand against the top of the frame, watching her.

Beth swallowed and looked away. "What can I do for you, Noela?"

"I'm just checking to see if you're coming to the launch of Trio tonight." Noela paused, then continued in a gentle tone. "I can't imagine what you're going through, losing Mr. Jordan, and we'd understand if you decided you'd rather not come."

Beth grimaced at the thought of attending the grand event tonight—the last place she wanted to be was with a huge crowd now Nico had turned her world upside down. All she really wanted to do was crawl into bed with a tub of chocolate ice cream. But she'd made a promise. "I'll be there."

"Thank you, Mrs. Jordan. I know the staff will appreciate it."

Beth hung up the receiver and poured herself a glass of water. She needed Nico out of here, now, before he found out about the festivities at the winery.

Knowing Nico, if he'd heard about the evening he'd have mentioned it by now, and she thanked the fates she'd be able to attend alone. This impromptu reunion was hard enough to handle without it being played out in front of one hundred of New Zealand's high society.

Nico pushed off the doorframe. He took three steps forward and leaned his hands on the bench on either side of her, trapping her with his body. "You walk away from me too often."

Heat radiated from him, reaching out and encircling her. Something she'd never forgotten about their precious time together was that she was never cold with him—his body heat had been enough for both of them when he held her.

Would it be so bad to close her eyes and sink into his heat now? To forget the crazy situation they were in and let herself have one more night with the man who still owned her unwise heart?

His breath was warm against her ear, and she heard

the moment it changed to a shallower, more uneven rhythm.

No matter what tricks her body was playing on her, she couldn't let herself forget this wasn't *her* Nico. This was a different man, one she had no future with. She couldn't survive their separation a second time. She might be protecting him by not telling the truth about her marriage, his son, his heritage, but she had to protect herself, too. Guard her heart.

She placed her palms flat on his muscular chest, feeling his racing heart beneath, and looked up into his unfathomable, black-lash-fringed eyes. "Nico, you have to go. You've got your apology, now we have to move on with our lives."

Slowly, he straightened. Then he smiled. "You're right. It's time for me to go. I know you'll need plenty of time to get ready for tonight's launch. Shall I pick you up at seven?"

The blood drained from her head. He knew! But of course he knew—the head office of Jordan Wines in Australia would know about any event one of the wineries held, let alone one on this scale. It seemed Nico was better at holding his cards close to his chest these days.

But she couldn't go through with her final performance as Kent's wife if Nico attended. Playing Kent's wife was difficult at the best of times, but with Nico in the same room, affecting her so intimately, it would be near impossible.

Nico would be a center of attention—there hadn't been a visit from Nico or Tim Jordan to this winery in over five years, despite their regular visits to the other Jordan Wines' estates. And people would be watching her, concerned for her. So any interaction between her and Nico would be witnessed by everyone present. Any undercurrents between them would be seized upon.

She schooled her features to casualness. "You don't need to put in an appearance."

"And forfeit a chance to honor my late brother? I wouldn't miss this for the world." He smiled with no hint of humor. "I did read the amendment to the program correctly, didn't I?"

The confident set of his shoulders, the raised eyebrow told her that he knew very well that the winery had changed the publicity for the launch of the new wine, Trio, into an event to both celebrate Kent's life and unveil what had become his final blend.

She moistened lips that were suddenly dry. "The seating arrangements and catering have been finalized."

"I sent an RSVP before I left Australia," he said over his shoulder as he strode into the receiving room and picked up his jacket. "Seven o'clock, or do you have to be there earlier?"

She followed, with rising panic scrambling her thoughts. She only had one line of reasoning left. "Nico, we *can't* go together."

He slid his arms into the jacket and straightened his tie. "Nonsense. We're Kent's family, they'll expect us to arrive together." He checked his watch. "It's two o'clock now, I'll be back in five hours."

In two steps he was beside her, dropping a kiss on

her cheek. It lasted a little long to be platonic, and his lips moved almost imperceptibly on her skin, but before she could react he was gone, shutting the door behind him.

Beth collapsed into the couch and dropped her head to her hands. The hundred guests attending tonight would include Kent's grieving friends and colleagues. Nothing improper could happen.

And her reaction to their embrace had proven one thing: if resisting Nico was her strongest line of defense, she was in deep trouble.

Three

The sound she'd been dreading came at precisely one minute to seven. Beth walked on trembling legs to the front door. She knew it was Nico—no one else could make a simple knock so commanding. As her hand rested on the brass knob, she took a last glance at herself in her full-length peach gown. It was hardly a dress of mourning, but she loved the skirt of gossamer layers and sheer sleeves in the same shade of peach—and she needed every thread of help she could get tonight to feel strong. Between the celebration of her late husband's life and her wildly unsettling escort, she'd be lucky to still be sane by the end of the evening.

She smoothed a trembling hand over the bodice, took a deep breath, then opened the carved wooden door.

In an instant, her mouth went dry. Nico stood before

her, tall and broad, wearing a tuxedo and a come-to-bed smile. The only time she'd ever seen him in a tuxedo before now was in magazine photos—when they were younger, he'd mainly worn jeans and T-shirts, the clothes he worked in at the vineyards.

But now he was a mature man, and the intense reality of the promise in him called to a place deep inside her, the girl she'd been and the woman she was now. His jaw was shadowed, despite having been freshly shaved. His thick, black hair, though neatly combed, still twisted in the rebel waves she remembered so intimately.

His eyes swept over her, and every square inch of flesh he touched with his gaze quivered, begged for his hands to follow, then his mouth.

"You're a princess." His voice was low, husky.

She couldn't speak, could barely think. Then he leaned in to kiss her cheek, and her eyes drifted closed to savor the feel of his lips as they lingered. In a distant corner of her mind, she was surprised by his tenderness but she refused to spoil the moment by dwelling on his about-face. When he broke the contact, her eyes opened and rested on his mouth.

"If you keep looking at me like that, we won't make an appearance at all tonight. Which is fine by me." His head angled and began another descent.

Without thinking, she raised her face to meet his kiss, then froze. *What was she doing?* She blinked once, twice, then pulled back, slowly shaking her head. This was a bad idea on so many levels, from Nico's coldness since his arrival this morning, to her attending the launch tonight—the winery staff had worked hard for months to put this event together, and since Kent was gone, the least she could do for them was attend.

"We should go." Her voice was a cracked whisper.

He lifted a brow, yet gave no other reaction, just stood there, filling the doorway with his intensely masculine presence.

Ignoring the heavy lassitude of arousal in her belly, she grabbed her coat and bag from the entrance table and closed the door behind her. Nico didn't say a word, but his eyes smoldered. She swallowed, then, knowing it was now or never, she headed for his car.

In the ten feet to the passenger side, he overtook her and held open the door.

Careful to avoid touching him in case she set off another sexual showdown, Beth slid into the seat then watched him walk around to the driver's side, mesmerized.

He moved with such a casual confidence, as if he was so sure of his place in the world. Yet, what would happen when she revealed the secret she held? He could lose that place, lose everything he held dear.

She swallowed around a lump in her throat. In some ways she wished she never had to tell him at all. He was the only man she'd ever loved. He meant too much to her to be unaffected by his pain. At least by waiting until his father passed away, she was saving him from heartache on that score…but only if she made no slips between now and then, and not let herself forget the stakes for even one moment. She had to ignore the fact she desired him like no other and keep her distance, stay out of his bed.

As he took his seat, he raised an eyebrow at her. "I told you to be careful about looking at me like that."

She dropped her gaze to her lap, trying to bring her emotions under control. Five years ago, she'd shared her every thought, her every emotion with him, but now was the time for self-discipline. If she let herself fall under his thrall again, she might ruin everything…. One lapse when she wasn't thinking straight, one careless comment about things that couldn't be spoken, and he'd know there was more. And he wouldn't rest until he knew everything.

He started the Alfa and pulled onto the private road around the vineyards. They traveled in silence for several minutes before he causally said, "Tell me about Mark."

The air leeched from her lungs. *Did he know?* His eyes remained on the road, as if he hadn't asked a loaded question.

"Why would you want to know about my son…Kent's son?"

He spared her a hard glance. "Regardless of my feelings about his parents, that boy is my nephew. There's nothing more important than family." He squared his shoulders.

"Nico—"

"Tell me about Mark."

Her hand snaked up to circle her throat. "He turned three last April." Luckily, she'd remembered to lower his age by a year to maintain Kent's story, and keep the secret of Marco's paternity safe for now. "He's bright and full of energy. He loves my parents' Dalmatian,

Misty—I suspect he's conned them into letting Misty sleep on his bed tonight. He usually does."

"Why doesn't he have his own dog?"

She owed Kent no loyalty, but she wouldn't speak ill of the dead. "It hasn't been…suitable for us to have a dog yet."

Nico's jaw tightened. "Kent wouldn't let him."

She shrugged. "Kent didn't like dogs much."

"Every boy should have a dog." He smoothly took a corner, then glanced over at her. "I noticed something strange at your house today."

Dear God, the trip from her house to the winery on the other side of the estate had never seemed so long. "You did?"

His fingers tapped lightly on the steering wheel and a frown line appeared between his brows. "There wasn't one photo on display of your son. I know Kent wouldn't send photos to our father, but none in your own home? That strikes me as odd for a woman who had albums full of us when we were together. And albums more of family—and *your* dog."

Her stomach clenched painfully. She'd rushed around and taken down all photos of Marco when she'd arrived home from Nico's hotel room. She knew chances were high he'd follow her—he always had when they had fought. He'd never let anything between them remain unfinished. Now she suspected he'd always follow, because he had to win. And the only way to protect Marco from this mess was to keep him hidden—in reality and in photos—until all secrets were out.

Kent had been careful that Nico or his father had never

seen a photo of Marco. The seemingly petty denial had been the last straw leading to the complete breakdown of his relationship with Tim Jordan—but completely necessary for Kent's twisted plans of blackmail.

She clasped her hands together in her lap until her knuckles went white. Just a weekend. Nico would be gone soon, and in a year or so all secrets would be out in the open.

For now, she needed an excuse. "I've taken them down and sent them away to have duplicates made for my parents."

"How thoughtful. I'm sure my father will appreciate his copies when they arrive." His voice was tight with leashed emotion. "It's broken his heart to never meet or even see a photo of his only grandson."

"Of course." She closed her eyes for a moment, silently cursing herself for not thinking of a better excuse. Naturally his father would want one—as would Nico. And then everyone's lives would explode....

Nico pulled into the driveway of the winery, and braked in front of the familiar and beautiful sandstone building now lit up with thousands of fairy lights for the launch.

Uniformed attendants opened their doors before one took the keys from Nico and drove the Alfa away. Nico's arm came around her waist. "Shall we?"

She wanted to melt into his warmth and solidity but that would be a bad idea at the best of times. Here, at a dinner to honor Kent's life, it was the worst of times. "I don't think you should touch me here, tonight."

He stiffened, and didn't remove his arm. "You belong to Kent here, is that your point?"

"It's not a matter of belonging to anyone. It's a matter of propriety. Of respect for the dead. Respect for your brother."

"Respect for my brother," he murmured, his eyes unreadable. Without warning, he swooped down and gave her one brief, hard kiss. It was over before she had time to react, but she knew exactly what it meant—he'd just reminded her that Kent was gone…and Nico was here.

She stood motionless, a little dazed, and glad now for the support of his arm at her waist as her body clamored for more—more of the kiss, more Nico.

Then he released her, stood back and swept a hand toward the entrance. "After you."

She walked in on unsteady legs, a little in front of him, and though she only looked forward, her whole attention remained riveted on the man behind her, as he'd no doubt intended. The kiss might have been devoid of emotion, but her entire body had reacted to the touch of his lips. Was *still* reacting, from the warmth rising under her skin, to her aching breasts.

But through her physical reaction, she had the worst feeling regarding the way he'd repeated her words about respecting Kent—he'd taken it as a challenge. What he'd do about it was anyone's guess, it was hard to know anything with this new Nico—he wasn't the openhearted, giving and impulsive boy she'd once loved. He'd become a rich, handsome, cold enigma.

One she was still finding difficult to resist, and more so by the hour.

As she stepped through the door to the function room already filled with guests, a huge display caught her eye. A photo of Kent dominated the room, twice as big as life-size. An assortment of flowers sat in baskets at its base, and tributes to his life and achievements lined the wall.

On the other side of the room was the publicity for the new white wine, Trio, a blend of three grape varieties. Arrangements of olive green bottles covered the tables and a banner of the blend's label was strung across the room.

The strains of modern classical music filled the air and open fires blazed in the six fireplaces built into the walls. The crowd was broken into small clusters of people, their conversations more subdued than at other launches she'd attended, but given the circumstances, she supposed that was to be expected. Nico had joined a group of three men in tuxedos on the other side of the gathering, but she knew he watched her from the corner of his eye. She felt it.

She looked back to the tribute to her late husband. The man who'd made her life a misery.

Noela, Kent's former secretary, glided across from a group nearby and grasped Beth's hands, offering a sympathetic smile. "We're so pleased you could make it tonight, Mrs. Jordan."

Grateful for the friendly greeting—a greeting without the hidden meaning Nico's words often took—Beth returned the smile. "Thank you, Noela."

"We asked Mr. Jordan if he'd like to say a few words about his brother, and he's kindly agreed. I know you're probably not up to it, but if you'd like, then you'd be more than welcome to speak, as well."

Beth's mouth went dry. "Speak?"

"About your husband." Noela squeezed her hands. "Only if you want to."

"Um, no—" Beth swallowed hard "—I don't think I could." She was having enough trouble keeping her secrets from Nico without having to convince a whole roomful of people that she was grieving for Kent.

"That's understandable, I knew it would be too soon. I'll just go and get everyone together for Mr. Jordan." After one final squeeze of her hands, Noela slipped away.

Beth's stomach twisted as she watched Noela pass through the crowd, pointing toward a podium at the front of the room, guiding people across. What would Nico say to these people about a brother who had tormented him his whole life? It was hard to imagine why he'd even agreed to speak—he could only have been thinking of Jordan Wines and keeping up appearances.

Her eyes sought Nico through the people milling about and found him near the podium, talking to Andrew, the acting winemaker. At that moment, Nico looked up, met her gaze and arched an eyebrow. Her pulse stuttered. He was planning something.

Noela took the podium and waited until the murmurings of the crowd died down. "Thank you all for coming tonight. As you'll be aware, we're not only launching our latest wine blend, Trio, but we're paying tribute to the blend's creator, Kent Jordan, who passed away recently. Kent's brother Nico Jordan has flown out from Australia, and has generously offered to share some memories of his brother with us tonight."

Polite clapping rippled through the crowd as Nico walked the short distance to the podium, his face appropriately somber.

He looked around the crowd, taking them in, nodding as he acknowledged their support. Then he found her, blinked slowly, and held her gaze as he began speaking. "On behalf of Kent's family, I'm touched that you've come here tonight to show your respect for my brother."

Beth froze. He'd opened his remarks with her phrase about respecting his brother. He *was* planning something. She folded her arms tightly under her breasts, hoping against hope he would behave decently.

"Losing Kent has been a tragedy to our family," his deep voice rumbled across the room, "made worse by our father being too sick to travel to the funeral. Since I stayed with him to offer comfort in his grief, I'm glad for the opportunity tonight to say a few words about a brother unlike any other."

Nico turned, making connections with people in the audience—a consummate public speaker. But she knew he was speaking to her tonight. She dragged in a breath, held it, on edge about what was to come.

"Kent was a formidable force, a man who always achieved his goals, letting nobody and nothing stand in his way. He pursued his beautiful wife with that same sense of purpose, not being deterred until he had his ring on her finger." His gaze speared hers and she almost swayed on her feet with the shock. She knew he'd planned something, but he'd dared to reference the way she'd left him? Sheer force of will made her stand taller and meet his gaze without flinching. Even though no one else would understand his meaning, it still galled her that he'd be so bold.

Nico continued in the same deceptively solemn tone. "It's tragic that such a young and strong marriage has been severed." Eyes from around the room turned to her, and she met some of them, accepting their sympathy, concealing the rising tension in her body.

"In fact," Nico said, eyes not leaving her, "I don't feel I can properly pay tribute to my brother without his beautiful wife here with me. Beth, if you wouldn't mind?" He held out a hand to her and the entire room turned, offering encouraging smiles, propelling her forward.

Her heart raced double-time, her hands were damp, but there was nothing she could do—short of rudeness—to avoid joining Nico at the podium.

She closed her eyes for a long moment, finding the composure she'd need, then the crowd parted for her and she walked to the front of the room. When she reached him, he pulled her close, placing a brotherly arm around her shoulders, but his eyes were full of the devil.

"Nico, please—" she whispered but he turned back to the crowd, some of whom were discreetly wiping away tears at the beauty and the heartbreak of the scene before them.

"The depths of emotion that Kent's dear wife and

I share right now can't be put into words." His hand moved from her shoulder to her neck, a kind, comforting move...except for the thumb that moved in sensual circles at the nape of her neck, hidden from the crowd, but sending shivers across her skin.

"Kent's death was a shock for all his friends and family. And for those of us left behind, for my father, Mark, Beth and me—" he turned and looked into her eyes as he spoke "—all I can say is that at a time like this, at least we have each other." He pulled her into a hug and the audience clapped their approval.

The embrace launched a flood of sensation in her body—her skin heated, her muscles quivered. This was so very different from the tender way he'd held her this morning—it was...*more*. More fervent. More intimate. More bone-melting.

And, it was lasting too long. An entire audience watched this embrace. She tried to discreetly push him away but he wouldn't budge.

"Nico, stop it," she said in his ear.

"But, my Beth, I'm enjoying it immensely," he murmured. "Why would I stop?"

But he released her and, still grasping her hand, led her away to another sympathetic round of applause from their well-wishers.

As soon as they'd cleared the main crowd, she whirled on him. "How could you?" she whispered fiercely.

"How could I what?" he said, low, as he nodded to a man across the room. "The winery wanted a touching scene and I gave them one. It'll be good PR for Trio."

"You know what I'm talking about." She narrowed

her eyes. "I hope you're satisfied with the show you put on."

One corner of his sensual mouth kicked up into a grin. "Actually, I'm not satisfied. Yet." He dug his hands into his pockets and rocked back on his heels, all cool unconcern. "I've had enough of the business talk and the homage to my half brother. One drink and we're leaving."

Leaving? They'd barely been here half an hour. She kicked up her chin a fraction and stood still. "I can't leave. This is to honor my husband. People are mourning here. I should be seen to be mourning."

Nico stopped beside her, his eyes narrowed, seeing more than she wanted him to. "But you're not, are you, Beth?" He smiled, smug at his realization. "There are no secrets between you and me—you had no love for him, never did."

She looked around. Too many people would be eager to hear this and make something of it. "Not here, Nico."

"Not here? You think *this* is going too far?" He moved closer, his eyes on her face. "Oh, *bella,* I could do much worse than this."

Her body yearned to move that last few inches and lean into him, ached to be held. But it couldn't happen, especially not here. "You said your speech would help the PR for Trio. If you create a scene, it'll undermine that."

He shrugged one shoulder, a casual, dismissive gesture. "You misunderstand the nature of publicity. If I hadn't said anything up there, it would have been disappointing for the guests. People hate disappointment. But you and I creating a scene…" His voice was low, beguiling. "The kind that's quiet, unobtrusive, but watched by every person in the room. Our guests would find that delicious and Trio would quickly become infamous."

This was about making Jordan Wines' guests happy? No, the predator in his eyes was too marked to miss. This was all about the two of them. About the simmering chemistry that was still between them despite how she fought it. She swallowed hard and took a small step back. "They won't have anything to watch if I walk away."

His hands snaked out and captured one of hers, holding it platonically between them, a concerned brother-in-law comforting the bereaved. But the heat of his palms made her skin sizzle, and sparks danced up her arm before heading to her core.

And he knew, damn him. The corner of his lips curved ever so slightly, relishing his victory. Though she was pleased to see he wasn't unaffected himself—the pulse at the base of his throat beat strongly.

He began a discreet sensual massage of her palm, her fingertips. "All I'd have to do is reach over and run one finger down your cheek, and I could have you in my arms. You still react to me, I saw that today."

Beth shivered. She couldn't let that happen. She disengaged her hand and took another small step back. "This night should be as sacred as a wake."

He glanced around the room. "I'm not sure if anyone here is mourning Kent—his nasty streak wasn't saved just for me. It ensured he never earned much respect or popularity."

"Be that as it may, this is still wrong." She turned and walked across the room needing as much distance from Nico as she could get. Because he'd hit the nail on the head—she still reacted to him. And that was a luxury she couldn't afford when she needed to hold secrets close to her chest for everyone's sakes.

As she took a proffered glass of wine from a waiter, Noela appeared at her side. "I wanted to check if you're all right."

Beth plastered a smile on her face. "I'm fine, thank you."

Noela leaned in, concern in her features. "You seemed very affected on the stage. I hope we haven't pushed you beyond endurance."

Beth held back a grimace and looked over at the back of Nico's head as he charmed a group of staff on the other side of the room. Noela and the winery weren't the ones pushing her limits tonight. That distinction went to the man whose broad shoulders looked like pure sin in his tuxedo. "I really am okay," she assured Noela.

After Noela left, she was quickly replaced by a stream of people offering their condolences and marveling at her strength in attending tonight. After twenty minutes, Beth was suffocating. She excused herself and walked out to the terrace, sipped her wine and looked over the moonlit vineyard. Below the distant twinkling lights of the town were rows and rows of bare vines. There was something comforting about the order of it, the neatness and…rhythm. She took a deep breath of the brisk night air and leaned the cool glass against her flushed forehead, glad for the respite from people, noise and the expectation of conversation.

"It's a striking view." The voice from the shadows was low and smooth and achingly familiar.

Beth wrenched around. At the end of the balcony, obscured by the dark, was a faint shape. If she hadn't heard the voice, she wouldn't have known for sure if someone was there.

But there was.

Nico.

Her heart tripped over itself as she nonchalantly leaned a hip on the stone balustrade that edged the terrace, facing him. "You've spent your whole life around vineyards and wineries. I'm amazed you still see past the hard work to the beauty."

"There's not much that's more beautiful than a fertile, lush grapevine." He paused and she heard the sound of a glass being deposited on the stone tiles. "Except perhaps a beautiful, lush woman."

Now her eyes had adjusted to the blanket of darkness, she could faintly discern his outline. He sat on the wide balustrade, his back to the view. She glanced over her shoulder to make sure no one else was watching before taking one step closer, flirting with danger. There was something about Nico being hidden in the dark that seemed deceptively safe. A dangerous illusion, she knew, and yet she took another step forward.

Simulating a casual pose, she swirled the wine in her glass. "I expected you'd be inside, working the room."

"They don't need me for that. I made the speech, the winemaker and other staff can take care of the rest."

She remembered the few events she'd attended with him years ago where he'd been happy to let others get the most attention. "You don't like the limelight, do you, Nico?"

"Come down here and I'll tell you the answer." It was the voice of Lucifer, tempting her with the apple.

"No," she said simply and sipped her wine. She'd come far enough.

"I think you will." She could hear a smile in his voice and it sent a frisson of heat across her skin.

"What makes you so sure?"

"Because you don't want to go back inside."

That was true. As much as she wanted to avoid another scene with Nico here at Kent's tribute, she wanted to go back into that crowd even less. She cast another look around—this was technically a public place, so nothing improper could happen. It had the added benefit of having no audience—he might have put on a show earlier, but he had no spectators for his wordplay out here. A public place that had no audience—it might seem like a contradiction, but it served as the best protection she could ask for tonight.

She moved down, to within a few feet of him. "Tell me about the limelight."

"Closer."

Even this close, she couldn't see him clearly in the blackness.

"I think here is just fine." She wrapped her free arm

around her middle and lifted the wine to her lips, taking the last sip.

"For now," he conceded and she could see the moonlight glint on his teeth as he smiled. "I don't seek limelight the way Kent did. I don't hate it, either. I don't have strong feelings about it one way or another."

"If you don't hate it, why not stay inside tonight and make use of it for Jordan Wines?"

He held out his hand for her empty glass and placed it beside his. "I had something on my mind and wanted space."

"Kent?" she whispered.

His eyes were strangely reflective, the predator that had lurked there earlier absent. "You."

He reached out and snagged her hand, dragging her closer, until she stood in the vee made by his thighs. A rush of heat pooled low in her belly, goose bumps erupted across her skin.

Head cocked to the side, he looked up into her eyes, his expression pensive. "Why are you on my mind so much?"

Their gazes held for an eternity and her breathing quickened. There was an honesty in his eyes that reached out to her heart, as if in the darkness of the balcony, the world could disappear and leave them cocooned in shadows. It was that dangerous illusion at work again.

Attempting to break the spell, Beth casually shrugged a shoulder. "Because you're here in New Zealand to see me."

"Not just now," he said quietly. "Always."

How she wanted to believe it was because he'd never

stopped loving her, but if that had been true, he'd have come for her. Would have at least checked on her after Kent took her out of the country. It was a senseless fantasy she'd only let herself have on dark, lonely nights—she knew if he'd come for her, her sacrifice would have been for nothing. It was far better that he'd stopped loving her when she left.

So instead she smiled and offered the only plausible reason. "Probably because I'm the only woman to walk away from you."

His mouth hooked up at one corner. "Maybe."

He laced his fingers in hers and tugged her closer still, into the circle of heat that surrounded his body. A shiver raced over her skin, as if her flesh recognized his was close.

"Nico, what was between us is long over," she said, knowing it was to convince herself as much as him.

"Really?" he asked lazily, and abruptly the reflective mood morphed into an electric simmer.

Beth began to step away, but he held her hands firm. "If it's over," he said, "why are you standing here in the dark with me?"

She could smell his clean scent, wanted to bury her face in his strong neck, but kept her voice even. "Because we were talking."

"Would you be standing this close to any of the men inside if you were talking to them?"

"No," she admitted.

"Would you let them do this?" He encircled her in his arms and brought her flush against his seated body, his chest against her stomach, his face in line with her breasts. Her breath caught at the hard, erotic feel of his erection pressing against her thigh.

"I'd say no, probably slap them." Her eyes drifted closed.

A hand crept up the back of her neck and brought her head down. "Tell me no," he said against her lips.

"No," she said and kissed him.

He tasted of wine and Nico and she couldn't get anywhere near enough. For one perfect moment, she was back five years ago, kissing the boy she loved on her back porch. Then he growled and nipped on her bottom lip, and she was jolted back to the present. Kissing this dangerous Nico was a new experience, in some ways more darkly alluring. She threaded her fingers through his hair, and he arched his neck back further to deepen the kiss.

She leaned into him, over him, resting most of her weight on his broad chest as she looked down into eyes as dark as the night that hid them. A shiver ran down her spine when he broke the kiss and watched her for a beat.

"Nico," she whispered, but wasn't sure if she said it aloud or if it was only in her head.

He kissed down her neck, pressed his tongue into the pulse point at the base of her throat, arms still holding her tightly to him, thighs closing to hold her in place. Trying to regain her breath, Beth looked out over the top of his rumpled hair to the distant lights of the town. They looked like a fairy tale. She looked down at Nico trailing moist kisses along her décolletage—if she was in a fairy tale, this was not the prince. The Beast, perhaps.

Gently, he slid one of the sheer sleeves down her shoulder, his lips following the path he created until he reached the top of her breast. He paused and laid his cheek against her, breathing heavily.

"Beth," he groaned, then arched his head back. She could no more resist the invitation than she could stop breathing; she leaned down and met his mouth, kissed him again, pressed her length as close to him as she could.

Voices near the terrace door sharply interrupted the haze she'd slipped into. They both froze as two women walked through the door. "Don't move," he whispered. "They won't see us."

"Oh, I know!" said a woman in a tight-fitting red sheath. "I just about cried when he hugged her up there. After all she's been through, I'm glad someone is looking out for her."

Beth felt Nico's grin against her cheek and now she did feel like slapping him.

"I wouldn't mind him looking out for me," a second woman replied in a high voice. "He is seriously gorgeous."

Beth felt a hot, moist tongue run along the arc of her ear before Nico sucked her earlobe into his mouth. Her knees wobbled but he held her firm.

"Isn't he ever?" Red Sheath said. "I'd buy as many bottles of wine as he told me to. They should have him on the label."

The joint sensation of gentle tugging on her earlobe

and Nico's warm breath in her ear was as bone melting as the kiss had been. Beth absentmindedly thought that the women at the door had no inkling of just how sexy this man really was.

"Look," the second woman said, "there's John Willis standing on his own. I've been dying for an introduction to him, come and talk me up."

The voices faded as the women rejoined the party.

Beth squeezed her eyes shut and sucked in a deep breath. She knew she should leave too or she'd end up doing much worse than making out on the darkened terrace. This time enveloped in the shadows was like a fairy tale. It wasn't real.

She pulled her sleeve back onto her shoulder. "I need to go back inside."

"I need you here," he said, voice rough, sending her pulse racing again.

Nothing in the world could be more appealing than Nico in a tuxedo, hair rumpled from her fingers, telling her that he needed her. But she couldn't stay.

She pulled together all the self-will she could muster to resist him. "Nico—"

"Okay, you're right." His eyes were as full of the devil as they had been at the podium. "Let's go back."

He stood and straightened his tuxedo, finger-combed his hair.

Wary of his swift about-face, Beth took a step away, but couldn't afford to waste the opportunity for a scandal-free end to this tryst. "I'll go first," she said, adjusting her dress and feeling around her mouth for smeared lipstick.

Nico wrapped an arm tightly around her waist. "We'll go in together."

Before she could protest, he led her to the large doors and over the threshold, into the edge of the crowd. He was all confidence and composure while she struggled to catch up with the abrupt change of both mood and scenery. One moment she'd been kissed senseless by Lucifer himself, the next she was again in the middle of her husband's wake.

He grabbed two glasses of Trio from a passing waiter and handed one to her, letting his fingers linger on hers a second too long. "As I said, one drink then we're leaving—feel free to mingle while you have it. I'll be back for you. Soon."

The heat in his eyes as he turned and walked away was unmistakable. He intended to seduce her, to make love to her, tonight. Her skin quivered and tightened, her belly felt heavy with desire still simmering from his kiss on the terrace moments ago.

Although, she corrected herself, lovemaking wasn't a part of his plans. He had sexual plans for her, yes, but they'd be fuelled by lust and passion alone. Not love.

And, shockingly, even knowing that was no protection. Fighting her attraction for Nico was as futile as it had ever been.

But…what if she gave in? Stopped fighting the inevitable? If she went to his bed, it would all be over by tomorrow. He'd leave never knowing the truth about Marco, about the blackmail…and she'd have one more memory of him to cherish.

Yes, her body whispered. *Do it.*

Under her clothes, her naked skin felt the caress of the soft fabric of her gown; the tips of her sensitized breasts strained against the bra cupping them. Every step she took, every movement, became part of a sensual dance.

She spoke to several winery and vineyard workers, sipping her wine as she mingled. Then called Andrew the acting winemaker over. "I'm so sorry, but I have a headache—it feels like a migraine coming on. I need to go home."

His face was a picture of concern, causing a ball of guilt to form in her stomach. "Of course—it's too soon. I can't imagine how you're feeling. As I've said before, anything we can do for you, let me know."

"Thank you, you're too kind." Her voice cracked with the force of her desire—she could *feel* Nico behind her, waiting. Fortunately, people would assume it was raw grief. No one could see what she was thinking, what she was about to do….

"May I call a taxi for you?"

She offered a small smile of thanks. "No need. My brother-in-law is here, I'll ask him to take me home. Please tell the other guests I wasn't feeling well?"

"Certainly."

She walked back to Nico and looked him calmly in the eye, determined not to give away how fast her heart pounded, not to anyone in the room—including him. "I'm ready to go."

He raised an eyebrow, surprised. His eyes searched her face again, and she felt the heat flash right through her. She knew what she wanted, and *he* knew she wasn't fighting it anymore.

Finally, he nodded. "Good." He took her hand and tucked it into his elbow, marking her as his—if only for tonight—as he walked her from the memorial of her husband.

Taking her to his bed.

Four

As Nico guided her through the hotel-room door and took her coat, Beth caught sight of the interior and hesitated.

Every surface was filled with flickering candles, enough to light the expansive room with a soft glow. Vases of out-of-season honeysuckle scented the air with their perfume, and—

And it was obvious he'd planned the whole thing. Had planned it before he'd picked her up for the evening. Before she'd agreed to come here.

Panic clawed at her chest. What was she doing here? She wanted him to make love to her, but she wanted it to *be* making love. *This* had nothing to do with love. It was unfinished business to him. Perhaps even some kind of challenge to lure her back to his bed.

The man who'd seemed reflective—emotionally exposed—for a few minutes on the winery's terrace was long gone. Maybe she'd imagined him. This Nico was the one who'd knocked on her door this morning, the man with a heart of granite and eyes alive with sin. She was out of her depth, playing games with the devil.

The tension of this moment, this night, this entire day, threatened to overwhelm her, but she couldn't let it. Praying some vestige of the Nico she'd loved still existed inside—the man who would have moved mountains to save her from pain—she turned.

She faced him with what she hoped looked like resolve, when it was anything but. "I've changed my mind."

He prowled toward her, his eyes glittering. "Are you asking me to believe you could walk away from this?"

He cupped her face and when she met his heated gaze the lines blurred, past and present and loss and need blending until even she didn't know if this would be heaven or hell—all she knew was it was inevitable.

He lowered his mouth to hers and she parted her lips without thought. His tongue plunged inside as he gripped her upper arms and she fell into the kiss, fell into him.

She'd been starving for him these long years, and now his mouth was on hers, she wanted more, needed it all. It was more than a kiss. It was coming home.

His arms crushed her into his solidness, held her tight, but not close enough, so she pulled at his bow tie, opened buttons and slid her hands across his scorching skin.

He groaned and shuddered, but didn't break the kiss. How had she lived without this? Apart from the joy of motherhood, she'd been a dead woman walking since she'd last lain with him.

Pushing the sides of his shirt apart, she touched as much of him as she could, relearning his body, discovering new planes and angles. His biceps were larger than they'd been, and she scraped her nails along their firm bulk, needing to know his changes. His abdomen felt as flat and hard as it'd always been, his skin as warm as she had remembered.

He pulled away, breathing ragged, eyes closed as if regaining control. Then he dispensed with his shirt and dangling bow tie in one motion. Her breath hitched. He'd always been magnificent, but now he was beyond even that. A Roman god far from home; a sculpture by an Italian master come to life.

There was a smattering of chest hair on his golden-brown skin where once he'd been smooth. She reached to feel, tentative at first, but then more boldly—there had been more changes but this was still the chest she knew. The one she'd loved so many times in her bed, in his, in the open air of the vineyard, in the barrel rooms of the winery late at night…wherever they'd found moments of privacy when their passion rose to undeniable heights.

She stroked across his pectorals, hungry for as much skin as she could touch, then lower, trailing her fingertips along the ridges of his abdomen.

"Your fingers have magic in them." His voice was rough, strained.

Lips like velvet skimmed hers, the darkly alluring taste of him engulfed her. His kiss was beyond the physical; it bordered a mystical experience, and she was powerless to do more than be swept along with its intensity.

Without breaking the connection, he unzipped her dress and the peach fabric slid to the floor, pooling at her feet. Then he wrenched his mouth away, captured her hands. "Just give me a moment to see you."

She arched her body, trying to make contact with his heat, his solidness…just him. Even touching his naked chest was more than she thought she'd be granted again in this life and the thought of it all being almost within her reach made her a little dizzy.

"Nico," she moaned, "touch me. Don't stop touching me."

With one hand, he unhooked her apricot lace bra and threw it behind him to land on the couch. He filled his hands with her breasts, cupping gently, rubbing his thumbs across their undersides. "Exquisite," he rasped. "Every square inch of you is utterly exquisite."

Then he knelt, and slowly—agonizingly slowly—he pulled down her panties. She leaned forward and ploughed her hands into his hair as he continued the measured descent of her last remaining piece of clothing. When he reached the floor, she lifted one high-heeled foot, then the other so she could step out of the panties, before he threw them to join her bra.

She was naked but for her three-inch silver heels and she reached for them to complete the task.

He stopped her hand. "No. They stay."

Past caring about shoes, she reached for his belt, but again his hand denied her. "Nico, let me—"

"We need to slow down," he said, his voice husky with want. "I've thought about this—*wanted* this—for so long, I don't want the experience to disappear in a blur of frenzied need."

She blinked. He was right. This would be their only night together—she couldn't afford to waste it.

She sucked in a long breath to steady her voice. "All right. We savor this."

A wolfish smile on his face, he picked her up and carried her to his bed, before carefully laying her on the satin quilt. He remained leaning over her for long moments, resting on fists on either side of her, his eyes holding a remnant of the tenderness he used to show her without disguise, and her heart caught in her throat.

Then it was gone, and, as he climbed onto the bed and positioned himself over her—but still not touching, the only emotion in his eyes was raw lust. The strength of that desire for her melted her inside and out. She quivered and clutched at his back, trying to bring him down to her. She'd been ready for him since she'd first opened the door to find him on her porch twelve hours ago. She'd been aching with arousal since he'd picked her up for the launch only four hours ago. And she'd been in an almost mindless haze of need since his kiss on the winery's terrace. Now she was well past ready to take him into her body, *needed* it more than all else.

"Now," she breathed. Her nails dug into his buttocks through his trousers, trying to draw him closer.

He didn't relent, even an inch. "You agreed. We slow it down." She pushed harder on his buttocks, not caring what she'd agreed to. He grabbed both her wrists, raised them above her head and secured them with one large palm, half his mouth twisted into a grin. "I won't be able to savor for long if you keep doing that."

His mouth dipped to hers, his tongue sliding between her lips with the confidence of a man assured of his welcome. Without her hands, the only greeting she could give was with her mouth, and by arching her hips up to meet his, still held above her like a burning magnet.

He groaned as her pelvis brushed his arousal, and he followed her as she sank back into the bed, grinding himself against her, releasing her hands to stroke down the side of her body.

The feel of his weight on her almost brought her to the edge. "Nico," she breathed. "God, *Nico*."

He leaned in, his free hand cupping her breast as he captured its peak between his teeth and tugging gently. The pulse at her core throbbed in the rhythm of his mouth; her body writhed beneath him of its own volition. Her mind was lost, her sanity possibly lost with it, and she couldn't bring herself to care. All that mattered—all that existed—was Nico.

His hand left her breast and traced a lazy trail down her ribs, across her abdomen, the coarse pads of his fingers generating exquisite sensations. She quivered with the desire that was alive in her belly, between her legs, longing to take him, to be taken.

His hand came to rest at the juncture of her thighs, dipping to glide across the spot that ached for him more than any other. A sound ridiculously like a whimper escaped her mouth, so she bit down on her bottom lip to contain further outbursts.

Nico's mouth moved across to her other breast just as one finger slid inside her, then a second, his thumb still caressing the point above them. He was assailing her from every front, overwhelming her with sensation.

Beth bunched the quilt in her fists, wanting more. The sensations he was producing weren't enough, but so *much* she was about to combust.

Breathing choppy, she reached to touch his chest, his arm, whatever she could connect with. She was dissolving, vanishing in a cloud of desire, rational thought had fled, only need for Nico remained.

She moaned, tossing her head from side to side, unable to stand another second. "Nico, please," she gasped.

Victory gleamed in his dark chocolate eyes for a split second before he lowered his mouth to the center of her desire and took her over the edge with his tongue. She exploded in wave after wave of tormenting pleasure, climbing higher still, to a place so blindingly high, nothing else existed. And through it all, she felt Nico's arms around her, knew she was safe, knew she was in the one place she belonged more than any other.

When she floated down slowly from far above the ground, sweet ripples still coursed through her body. Nico held her while she was limp and breathless until, awareness returning, she nuzzled into him. Then he discarded his trousers, rolled a condom down his length and with one, smooth, powerful motion, he was inside her. Air hissed through his clenched teeth and his eyes drifted closed. In the moment of stillness, she reveled in the feel of him filling her, joining with her, making love to her again.

Then he withdrew and, desperate, she couldn't restrain an incoherent cry of protest.

He lifted one of her knees, then gripped her foot still wearing the three-inch heel, and pressed a hot, wet kiss to the inside of her ankle. He lifted her leg to rest over his shoulder. Her body trembled at the eroticism of the move, but her heart beat powerfully for the man who looked deep into her eyes. They shared a connection, it'd always been unmistakable, but after this, surely neither of them would ever be able to deny it again. They fit together—belonged together.

He slid again into her slick hot depths, supporting himself on the strength of his arms, her leg over his shoulder moving in his rhythm, and within seconds she lost herself in his strokes. Her nails dug into the taut muscles of his back and he dipped his head to kiss her, their heated breaths mingling into one.

She was already so close to the peak again that for a moment, she tried to hang on, to make this last as long as she could… if this was all he offered her, this one night, then she wanted to squeeze every last drop of beautiful pleasure—every moment of this intimate contact with her Nico….

But his sensual invasion continued, took her higher, and his hand slid between them, to where their bodies joined, and with a skilled flick of his thumb her body imploded in sparkling glory, melding, merging with him, with the universe.

Within moments, Nico followed, then lay beside her, gasping for air.

"I don't think I can move," she whispered. Boneless, she didn't think she'd *ever* be able to move again.

His eyebrow arched. "You'd better recoup quickly, *bella,* because you'll be telling me you want me again very soon. All night long, in fact."

And when he reached for her, she surprised herself by moving to meet him, her recovery complete already.

Tomorrow she'd analyze how this night changed things between them, but here and now was for one thing only, and she met his kiss, his hands, willingly, ready for whatever he had planned.

Five

Nico woke slowly, wrapped around Beth. He blinked at the early morning sun slanting through the windows, feeling warm and content for the first time in years. Other women hadn't given him anything like this, nor had financial success.

He pressed his face into her neck, smelling her alluring musky scent. Beth and heat and sex and wanting him. God, he'd missed this. Missed her.

Ever since she sold herself to his brother.

The contentment he'd felt only moments earlier evaporated, leaving the dark, heavy ache that had been his constant companion for five years. The ache of betrayal. Every muscle tense, he edged away from her sleeping form.

He'd badly needed one more night with her, but

that had to be the end of it. He could never allow a relationship with her again.

Beth sighed in her sleep, nuzzling into the white pillow, her tousled pixie-cut hair partly covering her face. She looked so innocent as she dreamed in his bed, so vulnerable. A spark of doubt flared in his heart—*could* he walk away? Something in his chest shifted. Would she misunderstand their night together and expect more? Would she be hurt when he left?

He shook his head to clear it of worthless sentimentality. This was the woman who'd walked out on him without a backward glance. He would *not* let himself be fooled again. Clenching his jaw, he slammed the door to his heart closed. He wasn't the same trusting person he'd been. He'd made sure of that, had built barricades and fortifications around himself that no one had penetrated. And they never would.

Without making a noise, he slipped from the room, grabbing his trousers on the way. He dialed the concierge while he zipped his pants.

"Good morning, Mr. Jordan. How may I help you?"

"I'd like a cab." He glanced at his watch. Ten past eight. "To arrive in fifteen minutes."

"I'm afraid there was a big event at one of the wineries last night and all the taxis are on airport runs. I rang them a few minutes ago for another guest and they said there'll be a two-hour wait."

Nico swore low and hard.

"Would you still like me to make the booking?"

"No, I'll organize something else." He hung up and

rubbed his still-sleepy eyes with the heels of his hands. He should have thought of that—it wasn't as if he hadn't known about the function. Hell, he'd attended the damn thing with Beth.

He'd have to take her home. How could he face her after the night they'd shared—drive her all the way home, then say goodbye at her door? When he'd woken ten minutes ago, he'd come dangerously close to forgetting her betrayal—he couldn't make that mistake. A clean break—sending her home by cab would have been perfect.

He'd just have to create a clean break himself.

He stalked back to the bedroom, slid on a shirt and leaned against the door frame as he buttoned it. The sight of her sprawled under his sheets triggered his groin to harden for her again, bringing back memories of the night before under those same sheets. And in the shower. And against the wall.

He bit back a groan. It was over and he needed her gone ASAP—before he did something stupid, like crawl back into that bed and make love to her again.

"Beth," he croaked. Then cleared his throat and called again. "Beth."

She stirred and stretched and he clenched his fists to keep from reaching for her. Slowly, she sat up and the sheet fell to expose breasts he'd worshipped last night.

"Nico." One hand pushed her hair from her eyes and her lips curved into an uncomplicated smile. He tightened his mouth and watched the warmth and joy suddenly vanish from her expression and he knew she was aware things were different this morning. She blinked and gathered the sheet to cover herself.

He blew out a hard breath. "I'll drop you home."

She nodded, cynical understanding in eyes as blue as the ocean's depths. "Of course." She sighed, then cast a look around the room. "Just let me get dressed, or would you prefer to throw me out on the street wrapped in a sheet?"

He stared blankly at her. She was trying to get a rise out of him, but he wouldn't let her get the upper hand—she'd had it five years too long. Realizing his hand was clenched, he deliberately released it.

"Your decision." He shrugged to show her how little it meant to him. "I'll be downstairs, starting the car."

He grabbed his keys, phone, wallet and a jacket before slipping on his shoes. Then he walked out the door, not letting himself turn back. He *hated* that she still had so much power over him that he couldn't even trust himself to stay in the same room as her and not make love to her again. But in five long years, he'd never let anyone—especially a woman—have any power over him. Beth had taught him the danger in that.

He pulled on his jacket in the elevator down to the underground car park. When the doors opened, he strode over to the Alfa and thumbed the keyless lock. After sliding into the driver's seat, he began tapping his fingers on the steering wheel. How long would she take? Maybe she'd string out getting dressed to make him wait. To take back control. The old Beth wouldn't have done that....

His stomach dropped as he amended the thought—the

person he'd thought she was wouldn't have done that. How much of the persona she'd shown him had been real and how much fabricated? The question had tormented him to the brink of madness when she'd first left, but he'd buried it so deep that the only times he'd allowed himself to ruminate over it was when he woke in the early hours of the morning after dreaming of her....

The elevator pinged its arrival and annoyingly, his pulse spiked. If that was her, she would have done little more than slip on her clothes before following him. The doors slid open to reveal Beth in the peach gown she'd worn the night before, her hair not brushed. Desire stirred at her just-from-bed look, but he suppressed it. He couldn't afford to be distracted by lust now.

She walked toward the car, her heart-shaped face expressionless, as if she'd erected a wall of protection around herself as effectively as he'd done only minutes earlier. She sat in the passenger seat, head regally tilted, refusing to make eye contact with him.

Good. His hands tightened on the wheel before he turned the key and the car roared to life. He didn't want small talk, either.

They traveled the short distance to her house in complete silence, the mood inside his car icier than the cold winter morning outside. The town was quiet this early on a Sunday morning, but he supposed it was never as busy as any place he'd lived. Its lines of suburban houses were modest, yet charming in their leafy streets. They passed a small school with murals of laughing children painted down one side. Was that where his nephew would go to class? He pressed his lips together.

Another of his agendas for this trip. He wasn't leaving until he'd met the child.

In coming to New Zealand, he'd intended meeting his nephew, and this time neither Beth nor Kent would stand in his way as they had done since Mark's birth. The boy deserved to know his family, and as soon as Nico made contact, he'd ensure the next step happened quickly—his father, Tim, would meet his only grandchild as he longed to do. Nico would do anything for his father.

He pulled into the edge of the winery estate where Beth lived, then down her tree-lined driveway. When he reached the house, he left the car idling. He had a pithy exit line ready, but his attention was caught by another car and an older couple at Beth's front door. He recognized her parents immediately, as they waved across to his car. Beth had said Mark was with them this weekend, which meant the boy was probably inside the house this minute. Triumph surged.

Finally.

He cut the engine, got out and made his way over to the older couple, Beth rushing behind him.

Too late to keep him from meeting his nephew now.

He held out his hand to her father. "Mr. Jackson."

Her father didn't move as he took in Beth's disheveled appearance, then turned to Nico, his face a picture of rage and disapproval. "So you've come sniffing around again."

Nico withdrew his hand, realizing a moment too late that he was dropping this man's daughter home after having obviously loved her all night. Any father would be prickly. Nico squared his shoulders. "I want you to know—"

Her father's stance was rigid as he cut Nico's words off. "You abandoned our daughter when she—"

Tucking stands of mussed hair behind her ears, Beth inserted herself between them and grabbed her father's hand. "Dad, Nico was just leaving. We don't want to hold him up."

She glared at Nico—which was obviously supposed to be his cue to leave. Nico looked from daughter to father. There was something missing here.

Mrs. Jackson looked flustered. "We just dropped in for Mark's spaceship. It's his favorite and he forgot to bring it for the weekend."

"Nico," Beth said, eyes determined, "don't let us hold you up. I'm sure you have a million things to do at the winery before you leave."

He held her gaze and found something deeper behind her determination. Her eyes had always been so clear to read, at least to him, and even though she fought now to keep her emotions covered, he could still sense a smothered desperation. Desperation to stop him.

Nico crossed his arms over his chest. "Firstly, I'm not going anywhere until I've met my nephew—"

"Nephew?" her father repeated, eyes narrowed.

"And secondly," Nico continued, "I want someone to tell me what I'm missing here that—"

A small face peeped around the corner and lit up when he saw Beth. "Mummy!" He threw himself into her arms. "I forgot my space cruiser."

Beth picked the child up and held him tight, her

strawberry blond hair buried beside his mop of darkest brown. Nico frowned. That picture didn't seem right. He had always visualized Beth and Kent's child to be fair, like them….

His stomach went into free fall and only his iron will stopped him stumbling backward as the pieces of the puzzle clicked into place. It couldn't be possible, surely, and yet…

The boy struggled to be let down and when Beth complied, he grabbed his grandfather's hand and tugged. "Let's go, Granpa. You said we could go to the park when I got my cruiser."

Mark's eyes were the color of espresso, his face almost a replica of Nico's own childhood photos. Could it be possible?

His mind flew back to their last night together before Beth had left, making love in the vineyard, her body bathed in moonlight. To the nights before that. Had they used protection? Every time? Could this small child be the product of his and Beth's love all those years ago?

More than instinct told him he was right. Mark was *his* child, regardless of the age Kent and Beth attributed to him. Obviously a lie to keep him from the truth. To keep him from his son…

As the body blow slammed into him and the world tilted, Nico struggled to remain standing.

His son.

He had a child.

A small boy of his own flesh and blood. A thick ball of emotion filled his throat and he swallowed again and again, trying to move it. That perfect little person tugging on his grandfather's hand was *his*. He'd wanted children so badly when he was younger, had wanted children with Beth.

It seemed his wish had been granted—goose bumps broke out across his skin as he felt a sudden chill—it'd just happened without his knowledge.

Mind reeling, he focused on Beth. "We have to talk. Now," he said through gritted teeth.

Frowning, Mr. Jackson looked from him to Beth and back again. "You didn't know, did you?"

"No," Nico ground out.

For a suspended moment, everyone seemed shocked, either by the secret or its release. No one spoke a word or moved a muscle. Even Mark seemed to notice the unnatural stillness and froze, barely blinking.

Then, breaking the spell, Beth's mother leaned over to kiss her daughter on the cheek. "We'd better get going."

Her father held out his hand, offering the handshake he'd rejected only minutes earlier. Nico took the proffered hand and shook it once in recognition that this man hadn't been part of the conspiracy of lies and secrets. He was glad of that at least—he'd always respected Beth's father, both her parents.

He watched as the older couple bundled Mark into the car and drove away, too furious to dare look down at Beth.

Once they were gone and there was no chance of upsetting his son—*his son*—Nico turned to the woman who'd betrayed him on so many levels. "Well?"

In the distance, a falcon screeched as it flew up into

the blue sky, possibly disturbed by the car carrying their son. Trying to hold back her panic at the menace in Nico's voice, in his eyes, Beth's gaze was momentarily drawn to the bird.

Then, resigned to the confrontation that surely must follow, she drew in a breath of icy air and nodded. She turned and led him through the door into her living room.

They were barely inside when he spoke through stiff lips, his eyes cold. "I want a paternity test."

Beth felt her throat constrict. Of all the reactions she'd expected, she'd never considered this one. "You're questioning his parentage?"

"Of course he's mine," he all but hissed. "But you'll provide confirmation of the fact."

She nodded. It was a reasonable request under the circumstances, even if it hurt that he'd ask. "I'll call a lab first thing tomorrow morning."

Then, all pretence of control gone, Nico threw his arms in the air and words exploded from his mouth. "How could you keep my son from me?"

Beth stood her ground, refused to flinch but, oh, how could she explain the unforgivable? "If I'd had a choice—"

Nico held up a hand, eyes blazing. "We always have choices."

Every muscle in her body went limp. He was right. *She had to tell him, despite the consequences.*

At least part of the story—enough for him to understand. Heart racing, she walked on unsteady legs to one of the antique brown armchairs and sank into its soft comfort, trying desperately to compose words in her head. Words that had to make sense despite the trembling in every muscle and nerve of her body.

She took a deep breath and met Nico's eyes. "Kent blackmailed me into marrying him. I had to leave that night and never contact you again."

Two steps and he loomed over her, a wild intensity in his every feature. "So Kent didn't pay you?"

Money? She felt sick. How could he have believed she'd been for sale? Though how could he not, given how she'd left.

"No," she whispered. "All the money in the world…" Her voice trailed off as she felt the shame that he thought so little of her, when she still loved him.

Nico scrubbed both hands through his hair and dropped into the other armchair. "He told me that he bought you." But it was no longer an accusation; instead he seemed to be analyzing the information.

"I'd *never* be with a man like Kent if I had a choice. And…and I didn't know I was pregnant then."

"Would it have changed your mind?" His eyes zeroed in, trapping her with his demand.

Would it? She pressed her fingertips to her temples. Pregnancy or no, Nico and his father would still have been in as much danger from Kent's information. And yet family meant so much to him…. "I honestly don't know. Once Kent found out I was pregnant, he added that as another condition to the blackmail. If I told you about our son, or if I had any contact with you, or if I told you what he blackmailed me with, then…"

Her voice trailed off, but Nico supplied the ending.

"Then he'd make public whatever it was he was holding over your head."

"Yes," she whispered. And no matter how bitter and cold Nico had become, she couldn't be responsible for robbing him of all he held dear. Or robbing his father of peace in his last days.

He leaned forward, forearms on his knees, eyes hard and suspicious, obviously still unwilling to believe her completely. "Tell me what he had on you."

She'd known the question was coming, but still it sent a shiver down her spine. It would be so easy to tell him here and now, such a relief to share the burden she'd carried alone for five years. She licked dry lips, tempted almost beyond endurance.

But telling Nico he was illegitimate would be the ultimate act of selfishness. Robbing him of his family, heritage, career, *everything,* just so she could feel better? That would make her no better than Kent—not caring how actions impacted others. If she told him before Tim passed away, Nico would feel compelled to tell his father the truth, to allow his father to change his will—and stress could shorten Tim Jordan's life, according to the doctors. If Nico couldn't bring himself to stress his father, then their last days would be tainted by secrets not shared. How could she do that to either of them? At least if she held the secret for now, Nico and Tim's goodbyes would be untainted and full only of the love they shared. It was what they deserved, and she wouldn't let Kent's manipulations ruin that.

"Beth, tell me what he had on you," Nico repeated.

A hand crept up to circle her throat and she thought of

the letters, still hidden somewhere. After Kent's passing, she'd turned his bedroom upside down looking for them, before checking his office at work when she'd gone in to clear his personal items. The letters had been nowhere to be found, but she hadn't given up yet. She couldn't let them be found by someone else, just as she couldn't let Nico know their contents.

"I can't," she said, trying to hide the anguish it caused to deny him. "Please don't ask me that."

Nico flung exasperated hands in the air. "But he's dead! Anything you had to fear from him has expired."

She shook her head in jerky movements. She understood his frustration at the situation—she'd lived with it day and night for so long she barely remembered how it felt to be free.

She exhaled and met his gaze. "I can't."

"Why not?" The set of his shoulders, the way his eyes bored into hers, the twist of his mouth all proclaimed his distrust of her words, and she had no weapons to challenge it.

She closed her eyes for several seconds, searching for composure in the face of his onslaught. How to make him understand? To let her tell him only once it was safe? "Not yet. One day..."

"That's absurd." He waved a dismissive hand. "Kent is dead."

"I know...but—" She swallowed hard. "Nico, it's so much more complicated than it seems."

His jaw clenched and released before he spoke, as if gathering himself. "I won't stay away from Mark. He's mine. I wasn't giving up when I thought he was my nephew—now I know he's my own son, *nothing* could make me walk away."

Her heart glowed with pleasure that Marco's true father would fight for him even as it wept for the irrevocable damage in the relationship between his two parents.

Nico paced across the room and stood in front of the fireplace, which housed only ashes. The central heating had taken the edge off the air, but the fireplaces were what gave the house the perfect warmth and a sense of home. She hadn't been here overnight to stoke them. That it was now full of cold cinders seemed appropriate.

Nico leaned an arm on the wall above the brick hearth, his back to her as he spoke in a rough voice. "I've already missed his first steps, his first smile—I can never recapture that. Betrayal has cost me seeing my son learn to walk and run." He turned to face her again, eyes blazing. "And I've lost forever the chance to be the one to teach him to throw a ball. I won't pass up any other firsts."

His strong sense of family would never let him do anything else. Before this insanity had begun she'd dreamed of having children with Nico, and even then she'd known his commitment to those of his blood would be absolute. At the time she'd been thrilled by the thought. Now it was no less honorable, but the intensity of his devotion to family was bound to complicate everything dreadfully.

However, Marco would get to know his father, Nico would spend time with his son. It was the right thing to do, the best for both child and father. "I won't ask you to leave him behind."

But how would she survive being that close? Loving Nico and not having him. Wanting him and keeping a secret from him. It would be the worst kind of torture.

Her heart skipped a beat. "Nico, promise me you'll leave things between us alone. You'll have access to Mark, but you won't push me on details from the past."

His eyes widened as if she'd asked for the most ridiculous thing in the world. "I'll promise no such thing."

Oh, God. Rising panic squeezed her lungs. He had no idea how hot the fire he played with really blazed; she needed to make him see without giving away the secret that would destroy him. She had only one bargaining chip left. "Nico, please. Do it for Marco."

He paused, eyes scanning hers. "Marco? I thought his name was Mark."

Beth dragged in a shuddering breath and nodded. She owed Nico this information. "It is, officially."

She walked to a carved wooden chest and opened the latch, revealing the collection of photos that were usually displayed around the room. The ones she'd rushed to take down yesterday after visiting Nico's hotel. Part of her futile attempt to hide Marco's paternity a little longer.

With tenderness, she picked up a framed print of Marco running in the park with her parents' Dalmatian. It had always been one of her favorites, for the unbridled joy on her son's face, and for the way he resembled his true father in it.

She walked to Nico and handed it to him, a peace offering. "In my heart, and when he and I are alone, I've always called him Marco. He thinks it's my pet name for him. It was as close as I could come to naming him after you."

As Nico raised the photo, his throat worked up and down.

Tears filled her eyes, but she blinked them back—this was Nico's moment. "It was all of his father I could give him."

He dragged in a breath, then another before meeting her gaze, his eyes filled with resolve. "But now he will have more. Marco will have me," he vowed. "You've kept him from me for this long, don't even think about standing in my way as I get to know my son."

Emotion stung the back of her nose as she shook her head. "I won't, I swear."

Barely acknowledging her response, he continued. "And I won't be a once-a-year father. You'll have to share him equally."

He meant it as a warning, she knew, and she took it as one…but not the way he intended. How would she cope with the amount of contact required to share custody? To be so close to the man she loved, yet so far away.

A tear she couldn't hold back spilled over her lashes and crept down her cheek. "Nico, you have to believe I'm sorry."

His jaw clenched as he placed the photo on a coffee

table and stood silently before her, as if waiting for more.

Another tear followed the path of the first; she ached for him to take her in his arms and offer comfort. "These years without you, they've been my own private hell. Being married to that man—" she shuddered, swiped at her face, needing to say this, needing him to understand "—if it wasn't for Marco, I don't know how I would have survived."

Nico reached out and stroked her chin with his fingertips, but his eyes were filled with torment. Two sides of him were clearly warring. "He's gone now," he said, voice tight.

She looked deep into his eyes, wanting to believe there was more to his words, almost daring to dream it could be true. But then she saw suspicion still lurking there, and another tear broke free and slid down her face as she broke eye contact and looked at the floor.

Six

Nico couldn't touch her without wanting more—even the light caress of his fingers on her chin evoked a powerful and dark desire. He ran a hand down the length of her and felt her tremble. One night of Beth in his bed hadn't purged her from his system—and it seemed as if the feeling was mutual. He lifted her face, lowered his mouth and claimed her, sliding his tongue between her lips as he pulled her hips against his.

But he didn't *want* to want her this much. He'd exorcized his demons, had seduced her into begging for his touch again, and as soon as they sorted out arrangements for his contact with Marco and he found the papers his father wanted back, he needed to leave.

He knew now she hadn't married Kent for money, but if there was something in her past that Kent could blackmail her with, if she didn't trust him, Nico, enough to know he'd have helped her, then she still wasn't the girl he thought he'd loved. She'd been hiding something from him then, and his half brother had exploited the fact. They had no future and he needed to end this kiss.

Just one more touch...

His hands moved up her sides and over the soft mounds of her breasts. She moaned and slid her fingers across his chest, around his neck and his body demanded to be pressed closer, harder. Damn it, how could he leave her, leave this thing they had between them, and never touch her lush body again? He teased the peaks of her breasts with the tips of his fingers through the silky fabric, urging them into hard buds, wanting nothing more than to lay her down and have her.

Her fingers dug into his shoulders, griping him, before she broke the contact. "No, Nico. I'm not doing this again." She took an unsteady step back, her eyes filled with determination.

He smiled slowly, pulse in overdrive. "Your mouth says no, but your hands say something else entirely."

But he stepped back, reining his body in, giving her the space she asked for.

She refused to meet his eyes. "You have to go."

He quirked a brow. She could deny her body's need for his, that was one thing. But she wouldn't order his movements—especially when an issue of vital importance remained unresolved. "I'm not leaving until we sort out arrangements with Marco."

"Then you have to give me some space. I need..."

She gathered the skirt of her peach gown in her fists. "I need to change out of this dress."

Breathing still heavy from their kiss, she turned and rushed down a long hallway.

Nico scrubbed both hands over his face. Why was everything with this woman so damn hard? It was as if he had to go through six levels of hell to get anywhere. He couldn't keep his hands off her, couldn't forget her. Whenever he thought he had her pegged, she turned the tables—Kent hadn't paid her to leave, she hadn't wanted to abandon him that night….

But she had. And she'd taken his son and kept him hidden. Would she *ever* have told him about Marco if he hadn't stumbled across the truth?

He rolled his shoulders, trying to relieve some of the tension. There were too many unanswered questions, too many issues unresolved. Cursing, he followed her down the hall.

Outside the door, he paused, realizing what room this must be. Not just Beth's room, but the master bedroom. His stomach swooped. The last place on the planet he wanted to be was a room his brother had shared with Beth, but now, standing on the threshold, he was unable to leave. Morbid curiosity pulled him almost as strongly as the woman who'd led the way.

She'd unzipped the dress, and as he entered, she threw it on the bed and turned to the wardrobe.

He leaned back against the door frame, crossing his arms over his chest. "Were you ever going to tell me about Marco?"

She stilled. "Yes," she said without turning.

"Did you have a specific date in mind? Or perhaps once your luck ran out and you were exposed?" The idea of never knowing sent a pain rippling though him so harsh that he shuddered.

"I would have told you." She turned to him, her heart in her glistening eyes. "I can't say more now, but I promise you that."

Fool that he was, he wanted to believe her. Wanted to walk over and hold her close until her pain and his eased. Reason and experience told him that was dangerous, and yet, in this moment, he *wanted* to so damn much.

"How am I supposed to believe that?" he asked, voice no more than a hoarse whisper. "I'm serious, Beth. Tell me something I can understand. Believe."

Her eyes closed and a tear slipped through her lashes. "I can't do this now, Nico, I really can't." She turned back to the wardrobe and pulled out a pair of soft trousers and a sweater and draped them over her arm. "I'm having a shower."

An image of them together and soapy in the hotel shower last night flashed in his mind, juxtaposed with the current setting of her rushing into her en suite with tears on her face and him left in anguished confusion.

He thumped his head back on the wall behind him. It was probably a good thing she'd gone for a shower—he needed a little space himself to sort through the mess of feelings the morning had evoked. Before they got in deeper discussions about his son.

He wasn't walking away from Marco, but what sort of relationship could he reasonably have with a son in another country? School holidays in Australia as a minimum. And he could use the company jet to come to New Zealand for a couple of weekends a month. That barely seemed enough.

Restless, he moved to Beth's wardrobe. Adrenaline commanded his hands to move, to be doing something, anything. He blindly flicked through the assortment of clothes on hangers—an unusual combination of slinky numbers mixed with plain cottons. He pulled one out—a bloodred silk piece of nothing.

A dress a woman wore to attract a man.

Every muscle in his body tensed.

He opened the bathroom door and stalked into the en suite and held it up to Beth. "For a woman professing to have been in hell, you own an exorbitant number of sexy dresses," he said mildly, belying the irrational anger rising in his chest.

She glanced around the shower curtain and dismissed it with a flick of her wrist. "That's not a dress, it's two scarves stitched together with a belt."

He crushed the fabric in his fist. She hadn't denied his implication. The rational part of his brain told him there could be many explanations for this. Did it really matter whether she owned a sexy dress or not? Whether she'd moved on with her life?

His jaw clenched, grinding his teeth together. It mattered because she was playing the victim card in her dealings with Kent.

Besides, Kent may have been the blackmailer, but Beth was hardly blameless in the affair. She'd done something worthy of Kent's blackmail demand, and rather than have her dirty linen aired, she'd chosen to keep Marco a secret from his own father.

Hardly the actions of a pure heart.

He shut the door soundly, walked back into the bedroom, looked at the dress and had to acknowledge her assessment. So why...

Kent had bought it for her.

Nico thrust the red dress back into the closet, fury at both Beth and Kent churning in his gut. He looked around, searching for something of his brother to help focus his anger...but there was nothing. Not a single masculine item. He prowled further, searching for a sign of Kent.

The bathroom door opened and Beth emerged, red-gold hair damp, cheeks pink from the warmth.

He swept one arm to indicate her very feminine sanctuary. "Either you've expunged your husband from this room already...or you didn't share a bedroom."

She hesitated in the doorway, sapphire eyes locked on his. "His room was at the other end of the house. He never set foot in here."

Nico paused. "Even once?"

She pushed the damp hair away from her face in a move too studied to be casual. "He tried to persuade me to share a room at the first house we lived in, but I made it clear that although he had my hand in marriage, he wouldn't have my body. By the time we moved to this house, he'd lost interest. So, no, not even once."

Something primal reared in his chest. "I'm the first man to enter this bedroom?"

She shrugged one slim shoulder. "Yes. Unless you count the man who laid the carpets."

He took a step closer, but paused, not letting himself take that final step to her. The thoughts swirling in his mind wouldn't settle.

She'd stayed married to a man who hadn't fathered her child and who didn't share her bed. Kent must have had something big on her—she obviously had shady elements in her past and it was time Nico was let in on the secret.

He set his hands on his hips. "Tell me what Kent was blackmailing you with."

Beth paled, but she met his eyes. "I told you not to ask me that. You just have to trust me that it's something I can't tell you."

"Trust?" he growled. "That's a bit rich coming from the woman who succumbed to blackmail all these years—the woman who's been keeping my son from me."

She flinched, but her usual, infuriating air of dignity soon cloaked her features again. She raised her chin and kept her voice even. "I can't blame you for that. But you know me, Nico. Deep down, you do."

"That's where you're wrong." He stared hard at her. "I don't know you. But I do know your body…well."

He took a step closer. "I know the way your skin shivers when I skim my hands along it." He ran the back of his hand down her arm, and though it was covered by her sweater, he could see from the way it moved that she'd shivered.

He stepped forward again, so they were a breath

apart. "I know that when we're this close, your pupils expand, as if you can't bear to miss a thing."

Beth shut her eyes tightly, as if in pain, her forehead creasing. "Nico, this isn't a good idea. You know it isn't."

"I know that when I lean in, you'll smell sweet." He angled in to the curve of her neck, not touching, but close, and breathed her scent deep. It was almost enough to make him forget everything else in the world. The simple scent of a woman. This woman.

She raised her hands, bringing them between them like a shield. "Why put ourselves through this? It's just torturing both of us."

He reached out and grasped her hands, bringing them up to his face so he could examine them more closely. "I know these fingers." He kissed the pads of two fingertips, hearing the catch in her breath. His pulse picked up speed. "I know that when I kiss you—" he brushed his lips across hers, once, twice, then spoke against them "—you'll kiss me back."

He felt the war she fought with herself, the need her body felt versus the will of her mind. He kissed her again, lightly, teasing, then pulled back a fraction, daring her to come after him. She hesitated one second, two, before following his mouth and claiming it.

The heat inside him escalated, intensified. The feel of her lips, hungry for him, sent his blood quickening through his veins, and he lifted his hands to cradle her head, to hold her against the demands of his mouth.

It was long moments before he pulled back, breathing heavily, still holding her face between his hands. "There may be some changes from the years we've been apart, but I still know this face as well as I know my own," he said, voice low and husky.

He gazed down at her parted lips, now a darker shade of pink from his kiss. Need for her twisted in his gut as his hands ran a firm line down the sides of her waist. He wanted her—always wanted her—but he had to stay in control, not lose himself in her. Not ever again.

Beth laid her hands on his chest, rubbing slightly as if feeling the contours though his shirt and he closed his eyes, allowing himself to experience the sensation fully. He could bask in the effect her hands produced without losing himself—it was a matter of control, will power.

"Nico." The word was so soft, he wasn't even sure he'd heard it, but he opened his eyes, looked down at her. Her sweater pulled tight against her breasts with each breath she took. Gently, he hooked a finger into the vee of the neckline and dragged it lower, exposing the pale slope of her breasts. His heart damn near stopped at the sight. Such perfection—all of her was a perfection as he'd never seen anywhere else. He bent his head and placed a kiss on the skin that met the cup of her lilac bra, wanting more, needing more. Breathing against her skin, he pulled the fabric of her bra aside and his tongue swept across the beaded peak.

Her fingers combed roughly through his hair and she moaned. The sound sent electric currents of desire through his blood and he lifted her onto the bed where no man had lain...until today.

He eased down over her, lowering his weight, feeling

the exquisite sensation of her softness beneath him. Her breath slipped out on a long sigh, as if she relished the feel of his body pinning hers to the bed as much as he did.

Then, needing to move again, needing to be close to more of her, he eased the soft trousers down her legs, kissing the flesh he exposed as he did. "I'd recognize these legs anywhere," he rasped. "The length of them. The shape of this calf. The two freckles below the left knee." Once they were bare, he knelt between them and wrapped her legs round his waist. "And I know the feel of them around me."

The fabric of his trousers formed a barrier between her flesh and his, allowing him a modicum of restraint that he needed for now. He would not lose himself in her the way he had years ago—he'd believed himself in love then, but this was merely physical. If he ever truly let go again, he knew he'd risk his heart and that was unthinkable with a woman he couldn't trust.

"Nico, let me touch you," she said as she pulled his shirt free, then up, over his head. The feel of her fingernails lightly scoring his chest stole his breath away, and he rocked his pelvis against hers. When they'd been younger he'd wondered if he'd ever get enough of her, and even then he'd known the answer. No.

But he also knew the difference between wanting her body and losing his heart.

Beth undid his belt, and he leaned his weight onto one arm beside her, using his other hand to push his boxers and trousers down, away, free. Free to settle more fully between her legs. His skin pulled tight across his body, every muscle tense. He savored the feel for a long moment before reaching for a square packet from his wallet in his discarded trousers and sheathing himself.

When he pushed inside her slick warmth, she gasped and held his shoulders. He stilled and found his breath before moving.

Tremors ran through his body as she matched his rhythm. Some force inside him increased the pace, less a conscious thought than an inescapable demand of both their bodies.

"God, Beth," he groaned.

She dug her fingernails into his back and he felt his last thread of control snap. He'd begun kissing her as some attempt at claiming her back from Kent, but now he could think of nothing but her body as it encircled his, of her heat, of the sounds she made in her throat as she found her release, of the rising tide inside him that was close to crashing over the edge, of the brightness bursting behind his eyes an instant before he collided with the stars in the sky.

Blissful nothing was all that existed for minutes, perhaps hours. Nico held her flush against his body, their labored breathing synchronized. If there was a heaven on Earth, this would surely be it—holding Beth close after loving her body. When they'd been younger, they'd lain for hours after making love, sometimes sharing hopes and dreams, sometimes talking about nothing in particular, and sometimes the passion would rise again and they'd start over. It'd been a time when she was completely his—he didn't have to share her with work or family or other concerns. All they thought about was each other until they'd reemerge into the world again.

He stretched, looking around the room. But then the satiated haze began to lift and awareness of their present situation returned.

Nico silently cursed himself and rolled on his back.

There were so many reasons he shouldn't have slept with her again—yet when he'd been touching her, none of those reasons had made any impact. It was as if she wholly filled his senses, leaving no room for anything but her. Reason, doubt, even wisdom vanished. There was only Beth.

He listened to her still heavy breathing—it came from mere inches away, but may as well have been forever. Something in his gut twisted.

He'd wanted to claim her back from Kent, but he'd claimed nothing. It'd been an empty gesture. They had no future—she continued to keep secrets from him, would still be keeping his son from him if he hadn't seen him with his own eyes.

At the thought of his son, his chest clenched tight. That was the person he should be focusing on. The one he should have been claiming back from Kent.

He rolled toward Beth. "I want to meet my son."

Seven

Beth trembled with the effort of controlling the maelstrom in her heart. Her body still glowed from his lovemaking and yet he'd turned so quickly to making demands.

Perhaps she didn't know him at all anymore. Her nose stung with unformed tears. Why did she keep trying to turn him back in her mind—back into the man she'd known? He'd changed immeasurably, and she had no way of anticipating or even understanding his behavior anymore.

A sickening thought crept into her mind—had he made love to her as a tactic? Part of a plan to gain access to Marco?

She laid an arm across her eyes. No, he didn't need to. Nico was right—he *did* have a right to meet Marco properly. And her beautiful son would unquestionably benefit from the input of a man who was truly interested in him. One who wouldn't cause him to ask, "Why doesn't Daddy want to play?" or "Why doesn't Daddy love me?" as Marco had done of Kent. Those words had cracked her heart wide open.

There was no denying that this introduction was the right thing to do, the best thing to do—what she'd dreamed and secretly hoped would one day happen.

Except, in her fantasies, she'd had time to plan the event, ensure everything would be perfect. Time to prepare Marco so he was in a relaxed, receptive mood. Organize food and distractions to avoid any awkward silences. This first meeting would be the foundation of their future relationship. A rushed, impromptu encounter risked too much.

And Nico was in such an unpredictable mood. Would Marco pick up on the underlying tension that still sat between his parents?

She looked into Nico's eyes, burning with tightly leashed emotion. His need to meet his son wrapped around the pieces of her broken heart and squeezed until she could barely stand the pain.

He reached across her to lift the handset from the phone beside her bed. "Ring them."

She focused on the phone held in his long, bronze fingers. "I'm not sure it's the best time."

"You're forgetting," he said, voice firm, "he's my son, too. Decisions regarding Marco are no longer yours alone."

Again, he was right. But there was so much riding

on this first meeting. She met his gaze. "Let me arrange something more planned. Introduce the idea to Marco first."

Something changed in his eyes, almost as if she'd wounded him. "Do you question my ability to bond with my own son?"

Truth was, he'd always had a knack with children. He loved kids and they usually loved him back. She'd once watched him spend hours teaching his cousin's six-year-old daughter, Georgia, to hit a tennis ball, and an entire morning charming a class of ten-year-olds on a school tour of the vineyard.

She had to admit, Marco would probably adore him. And Nico would put aside his feelings for her and relate to Marco on their child's terms. Not an easy thing for any man who'd been deprived of his son all these years, but she knew he'd handle it and remain unaffected in front of Marco.

But she couldn't throw everything at Marco in one go. So she'd lay down one condition. A deal breaker.

She wriggled to sit up, leaning against the headboard, and clutched the sheet to her chest. How to phrase this? Though, it probably didn't matter—Nico was going to hate it however she worded her conditions.

"I need you to agree to something first."

In one smooth motion of his powerful arms, he'd sat up against the headboard, as well, a skeptical eyebrow arched. "Another delaying tactic?"

Beth ignored the barb; she couldn't afford digressions now. She lifted a hand to touch him, to soften the blow, but dropped it again. Nothing could soften this. She just had to say it. "Nico, you can't tell Marco you're his father yet."

His face froze. Then his eyes slowly narrowed. "You won't deny me that."

The blood in her veins pounded its way through her body, but she wouldn't let her voice waver. "As you pointed out, he's never met you properly, just seen you briefly this morning."

She gathered the blanket around her, partly against the chill in the air, partly in response to the chill in Nico's eyes. She had to keep her son's needs at the forefront of her mind. "How do you think he'll feel with this dropped on him—especially after his first time dealing with death only a couple of weeks ago?"

She remembered Marco's tiny body racked with sobs when Kent died. Despite all the neglect, Marco had loved the man he believed was his father.

A seed of doubt lodged in her chest—was it too soon to expose Marco to this? She pictured his beautiful face in her mind, so happily leaving with her parents this morning for his weekend sleepover. No, she knew her son, and he was resilient—he'd cope as long as she stepped carefully. And if she could make Nico understand.

She rolled onto a hip so she could face him more squarely. "This isn't about you or what you need. It's not about me. This is about a four-year-old boy—a small boy who needs time." She drew in a breath. "His world is too unstable to throw surprises at him."

Nico crossed his arms and looked at her impassively. But he was considering it, she could tell. It was in the way his index finger tapped lightly on the elbow it rested on. Strange how some things about him had changed so much and others were exactly the same.

Then he uncrossed his arms and scrubbed a hand through his ruffled hair. Decision made. "So how do you propose we play it?"

She breathed out a sigh of relief and offered him a grateful smile. "You can meet him today and then in the next couple of days sometime I'll tell him that you're his father. Then he'll have a face to your name, and we won't be putting him on the spot."

Nico rubbed a finger across his frowning brow. "So I pretend I'm nothing to him?"

Her heart missed a beat at the flash of raw vulnerability he couldn't quite hide. Others may have missed it, but it was as clear as the shining sun to her.

She softened her voice. "He thinks Kent is his father, and he knows your name as his uncle. It'll have to be enough for today."

Nico gave a curt nod, but the storm clouds in his dark brown eyes betrayed his true feelings. And she understood the desperate need of a parent to hold their child, to proclaim to the world that this was their own flesh and blood. But it would be soon—as soon as she was sure Marco was ready.

She took the phone, dialed the number and waited until her mother picked up. "Hi, Mum, it's me."

"Hello, darling. Is everything all right?" she asked with a sharp edge to her voice. "That was so awkward this morning, I wasn't sure if we did the right thing in leaving."

Beth darted a glance at the man who still lay beside her in her bed, watching, listening. She swallowed. "I'm fine. Everything's fine."

"You can't talk. He's still with you, isn't he?"

She rolled over to face the wall, even knowing it made little difference. "Yes. Look, are you in the middle of anything with Mark? Because I'd hoped you'd bring him to meet…his father."

Her mother exhaled slowly and she could just imagine her patting down her short gray hair. "So it's all out in the open now. What's your plan?"

Beth closed her eyes. "Mum, can we talk about this later?"

A resigned sigh came down the line and she knew she hadn't heard the last of the topic, but when she spoke there was a comforting smile in her mother's voice. "Okay, sweet pea. You want us to bring Mark to the house?"

She opened her eyes and scanned the room, visualizing the meeting. Not the house. She needed somewhere more neutral, more fun for Marco so he was in the most receptive frame of mind. "How about the playground at the winery?"

"Sure. We can be there in fifteen minutes."

"Thank you. And, Mum, don't mention anything about Nico to him. I'll explain to Mark when you get there."

She set the phone back into its cradle and felt Nico's eyes never leave her face. "They're on their way to the winery playground."

"Good. Let's go," he said, already stepping from the bed.

They dressed quickly and headed for Nico's Alfa. Beth was a jumble of nerves, badly wanting this to go well for everyone's sake.

"Is there anything I should know?" Nico asked quietly as his car purred away from her house.

Beth tensed. Was he asking if she'd kept more secrets? Had he guessed that the secret she'd allowed herself to be blackmailed with was about him? She looked out over the tall trees that lined her driveway before answering. "Like what?"

"I don't know." He frowned and he gripped the steering wheel more firmly. "Marco's favorite game. If he has any allergies. Whether he hates being tickled."

She relaxed and bit down on a tender smile. He wasn't accusing her of anything—he wanted to be prepared before meeting his son. The way he'd prepare for any other important meeting: gathering information.

She looked across at her son's father, wanting to smooth a rebel wave that had fallen onto his forehead, but restraining herself. Instead, she gave him the information he wanted. "His favorite game is chasey. He's lactose intolerant but I don't foresee that coming up at the park. He adores being tickled, and also tickling someone else."

Nico nodded at each new piece of information as if filing them away, then paused as he turned the wipers on to clean the windscreen.

He cast her a quick glance. "There must be more you can tell me," he said solemnly.

"You won't need it, Nico," she said putting her heart into her words. "He'll love you."

Nico nodded again, his chest expanding as he took a long breath, but didn't say anymore. They traveled the rest of the familiar road to the winery in silence and when they arrived at the playground, her parents were already sitting on a park bench, watching Marco run with Misty the Dalmatian.

Nico came around and opened Beth's door, but instead of closing it when she got out, he stood watching Marco running in figure eights, Misty close behind with her tail wagging madly.

Nico's throat worked up and down. "He's mine," he said softly.

Beth slipped her hand into his and Nico gripped it tightly. Despite everything they were at odds about, in this they were united—wonder at the miracle of a small boy.

Marco whooped and fell to the ground, giggling, his woolen hat slightly askew. Misty stood over him, licking his face wherever she could, eliciting more laughs from their son.

Nico cleared his throat, but still his voice was husky. "He's perfect."

"Yes," she whispered. The product of their love. Nothing had ever been more perfect than this small boy.

Then he released her hand and took a deep breath. "I want to meet him."

Beth nodded. As they walked across the manicured grass to the bench, she tried to convince herself that this meeting wasn't important, momentous. Marco was just meeting his uncle. But it was so much more than that— first impressions counted, and this would be Marco's first interaction with his father, whether or not he knew it now.

Beth's parents both stood and shook Nico's hand, and Nico asked questions about the seasonal weather on the South Island. The ease of his conversation starkly contrasted with his every contact with her in the last two days. He smiled and charmed them—the perfect son-in-law.

Kent had tried to build a rapport with her parents, back when he'd thought he had a chance of making theirs a real marriage, but neither her mother nor father had ever warmed to him. Unlike their enthusiastic responses to Nico's comments now.

But, despite being the father of their grandson, Nico would never be their son-in-law.

Damming the emotions before they could overwhelm her, Beth turned away from the scene and called to Marco. He threw his head up and came running, his brightly colored scarf flying behind him. When he reached them, he launched himself at Beth's legs. "Mummy, I was chasing Misty!"

Her heart swelled to fill her chest and she hugged him tight, savoring his cold cheek pressed to hers, his warm breath on her skin. How she wished she could have protected him better from the mess she'd been in during his short life. And from an uncaring, false father. But most of all, from missing out on having a real father. Something all the money in the world couldn't buy.

Something that would hopefully be rectified, starting today.

Marco wriggled from her grasp and whispered, "Mummy, who's that man?"

Beth looked around and saw her parents had moved back to the cars, giving them some privacy, and leaving Nico standing alone, watching them with his hands in his pockets.

Then, in two long strides, he was beside her. "I'm your Uncle Nico from Australia."

Marco smiled shyly up at his father.

Nico crouched down to be at Marco's eye level. "Hello, Marco."

"Have you seen a kangaroo?"

Nico laughed. "As a matter of fact, I have." Misty came over to sniff Nico's shoes and Nico casually rubbed behind her ears. "I see you like dogs."

Marco nodded earnestly. "Misty is my best friend."

"I'm going to buy you another best friend. Your very own dog. Would you like that?"

"Yeah!" Marco threw himself into Nico's arms.

Beth's heart melted like warm honey. Marco rarely took to strangers so quickly, but then this man was his father, even if he didn't know it yet. Was there perhaps a subconscious connection between them? Or was it Nico's natural charm at work again—he always got whatever he wanted...including her in his bed again.

Then Marco pulled back, looking from her to Nico, his dark chocolate eyes so similar to his father's. "But what about Misty? She'll miss me. She loves me, Granpa says so."

Nico smiled. "I can tell she loves you a lot. But you can still visit her, and she might like another dog to play with, too. They could be friends."

"Yeah, friends!" Marco grabbed Beth's hand. "Mummy, Uncle Nico's gonna buy me and Misty a dog!" His eyes shone with such pure and innocent joy that she barely resisted hauling him close again.

Nico looked up and snared her gaze, challenging. She knew he was waiting to see if she countermanded him about the dog. But she wouldn't. She'd wanted Marco to have a dog. Kent had been the one to veto the idea whenever she'd brought the subject up. He'd had a ready supply of excuses—it'd shed on the carpet, it'd be too much work—and no amount of pleading from Marco could change his mind.

Getting a puppy had been on her list of things to do in the last few weeks, but if the new dog came from Nico it had the extra advantage of sealing Nico firmly in his son's affections. It was a great idea.

She nodded to Nico before placing a hand on her son's head. "I heard. That will be wonderful."

Marco smiled up at her, then his eyes widened like they did when he had an idea and he whirled to Nico so fast his hair spun out. "We could go tomorrow."

Nico chuckled but shook his head. "I have a plane to catch in the morning, so I won't be here when the shelter opens. But I promise I'll arrange something very soon."

Satisfied, Marco grabbed one of Nico's broad hands in his two small palms and tugged. "Wanna come see the slide?"

Nico stood in one easy motion and followed Marco to the slippery slide. Marco ran to the ladder and climbed, and Misty put her paws up on the second rung, as usual wanting to follow her playmate.

"Catch me, Uncle Nico!" Marco slid down, straight into the strong, bronzed arms waiting for him. Nico swung him up into the air, eliciting delighted squeals.

Nico was obviously entranced—though his smile was shadowed, it was also wide, something she hadn't seen since he was twenty-four. The wind ruffled his dark hair and his trousers pulled taut over his muscled thighs as he crouched, ready to catch Marco again.

God above, she loved him.

It was a love so deep that she had no idea how she'd survived without him. Just seeing him here was nourishment to her soul. But that deepest of loves was exactly the reason she'd left with Kent. No force on Earth could have made her stand by and do nothing as the man she loved was wounded.

Her mother tapped her shoulder. "Here, darling, why don't you lay these out?" she said, passing her two blankets.

Beth turned to see her mother had brought baskets of food for a picnic and she and Beth's father were in the process of unloading the car.

A rush of gratitude for her parents' thoughtfulness brought an appreciative smile to her face. They'd had little warning, yet had packed bread, fillings, drinks, cakes and fruit for an early lunch. Beth laid the blankets on the grass and helped to set the food out before catching her mother in a quick hug.

"Thank you, Mum."

"It was nothing," her mother replied, smiling. "We were planning a picnic anyway, so we already had the baskets packed. I just added a few things so there was enough for two more. We thought you and Nico might not have had a chance to eat yet…." Her voice trailed off in question.

Beth thought back over the morning, from their early arrival at her house where Nico first saw his son, to Nico loving her body less than an hour ago. There hadn't been a spare minute for food.

Her eyes drifted to Nico who was crouching to catch her sweet boy again. "No, we haven't eaten yet," she told her mother without turning. In a haze of warmth, Beth watched the two people she loved most in the world playing on the slide.

"You know," her mother said, "I always had a lot of time for that young man."

Beth bit down on her lip to stop it trembling with the emotion that threatened to overwhelm her. "I know," she whispered.

Her mother patted her arm and walked away, and Beth stole a few more moments of watching Nico and Marco before calling them over.

Lunch was eaten to the sound track of Marco giving his dad a condensed history of his relationship with Misty, a list of his favorite books and what toys he owned. Nico listened attentively, occasionally catching Beth's eye in shared humor about something Marco inadvertently said. Those moments were beyond compare. Kent had never had any interest in parenting

Marco, so she'd had no experience of sharing the simple beauty of her son's thoughts with someone besides her own parents. And for it to be Marco's father sharing this with her made it perfection itself.

When her mother suggested it was time for them to leave, Beth was surprised to see how the time had flown by.

A big part of her wanted to keep Marco with her for the rest of the day, but this weekend sleepover at his grandparents' had been planned ever since the date of last night's launch had been set. She knew her parents had surprise tickets to a movie that started in an hour; it'd be selfish to take him now, no matter how much she needed the comfort of her son nearby.

She called Marco over and helped buckle him into her father's car, with Misty on the seat beside him, her own car restraint already in place.

Nico moved away, oddly giving her a moment of a private farewell to her parents and son, and she was grateful. She needed the time to center herself, to rein in rushing thoughts—like when Marco would be ready to hear the news about his true father. And where that left her relationship with Nico—would shared parenting of their son be all they ever had together?

Imagine being that close to him and not having him. Beth crossed her arms tightly under her breasts.

After the car rounded a corner and disappeared, Nico turned to her. "We have some things to talk about."

She knew they did, but something in his tone made suspicion prick at her senses. "We can go back to my place if you like. Or to your hotel?"

He shrugged one shoulder. "Here is fine."

In a playground? She cocked her head to the side as she examined his strong features—they gave no clues. This was obviously important, so why discuss it in a child's playground? Perhaps some sort of snap decision he'd made and he didn't want to wait before telling her? Goose bumps rose on her skin.

She looked around at the grassed area and vacant play equipment. They could walk over and sit on the swings for this conversation but it would probably be better to just stand where they were. She turned to him, wariness straightening her spine. "What do you want to say?"

"We'll get married as soon as I can arrange it." His voice was neutral, his face still inscrutable.

Beth's stomach lurched and blood roared past her ears. For the second time in her life, one of the Jordan brothers was demanding she marry him. Only this time was worse. It was the brother she'd dreamed would lovingly propose one day. Over the years, in quiet, secret moments, she'd fantasized Nico would find her, lay his heart out and ask for her hand in marriage. *That* proposal wasn't on the table. Likely it never would be.

She licked parched lips and took a breath. "Why?"

He met her gaze calmly. "Marco needs to have two parents."

"He *has* two parents."

Nico crossed his arms over his chest and rocked back on his heels, assured, confident of getting whatever he wanted. "He needs two parents in the same house, both actively involved in his life."

Her heart was racing too fast, but she had to stay in

control, to logically counter Nico's arguments. Marriage under these conditions was out of the question.

The breeze blew strands of her short hair across her face; she smoothed them away and tucked them behind her ears. "He can have us both actively involved without us being married or living together."

"I won't compromise on this." Nico waved away her objection with a flick of his hand. "He needs us to be married."

Riled, she felt her jaw clench at his attitude. "Don't tell me what he needs. I'm his mother. I know him."

Nico speared a glance at her. "So far you've given him Kent and kept him from a grandfather and father who would love him."

Beth opened her mouth to reply, but no sound came out. His dart had hit its target—where the guilt for what she'd done swirled in her belly. She placed a hand over her stomach and waited a moment until her voice was strong. "I understand your point. But I've been a good mother."

"And I would have been a good father," he said quietly but fiercely, fists curled tightly at his sides.

"You would have made the best father in the world back then, no question." She swallowed past the sadness and guilt and grief. "And I'm more sorry than you can know that things have happened this way because they've changed you."

"What do you mean?" he demanded.

Beth looked around at the playground, trying to assemble her thoughts. Another family had come to play on the equipment. A mother, a father and two little boys.

A *family*. Her eyes stung with emotion at the sight of them laughing easily, of the parents' shared joy in their children.

If she married Nico, she'd create a false family. Again. A lie that would break her heart every single day.

She took a step back, creating both physical and emotional space between them. But she needn't have bothered—they'd already severed the ties that had once bound them more tightly than any vows of matrimony.

She felt cold everywhere, across her skin, deep down in her bones, but she faced him and lifted her chin. "I won't marry you, Nico. I won't sell out again and give myself to a man who doesn't love me. Even if it would mean Marco having his father in the same house." It would destroy her inside when she loved him more than ever.

At least she'd been able to close her heart to Kent, keep herself protected. She'd have no such defense against Nico day in, day out. More than anything, Marco needed his mother to be emotionally whole so she could give him a stable and happy home. It would not be best for Marco to have both his parents in the same house and be constantly exposed to the tension she and Nico would create in each other's presence.

Nico looked over at her. "You won't marry me?" His voice was raw, his face dismayed.

Beth stilled. Was this just about Marco? Her heart hammered in her chest as she contemplated the unthinkable. Could a remnant of Nico's love for her have survived the past five years?

She understood he was reeling from meeting his son for the first time; it was unsurprising he'd overreacted. But, perhaps what he'd proposed as a marriage of convenience could be something more.

She still loved him, there was no question of that. And if, in spite of everything, he had feelings for her buried down deep, could they make this work? She remembered his unguarded words on the terrace at the launch.

Why are you on my mind so much? Not just now, always.

Maybe she was unwise for still hoping. Maybe she was fooling herself. But maybe there was a genuine chance they could have a real family.

There was one thing she knew—she had to make sure. Had to ask the question before she ruled the possibility out forever.

Eight

Heart thudding so hard he could almost feel his whole body reverberate with each beat, Nico reached for the aviator sunglasses resting on his head and slid them down to shield his eyes against the bright winter sun and the woman in front of him.

She wouldn't marry him.

Beth would live with his son, while he lived…elsewhere.

Restless, he looked around, needing to do something with the adrenaline surging through his body. The playground sat beside the winery, but on its other three sides it was bordered by the vineyard.

"I'm taking a walk," he said, trying to keep his voice from a growl.

Beth nodded, tense but seemingly unruffled by his decision. "I'll come with you."

Acknowledging her company with a curt nod, he walked to the edge of the expanse of bare vines and down the first row. Her refusal churned over in his head as he walked, feeling like it pounded behind his eyes.

He would not abide being a weekend father.

Now that he'd met Marco—made a genuine connection with him—he couldn't imagine not being in his life every day. He was a great kid, that was obvious, and he needed a father to teach him things. Not just throwing a football on weekends, but everyday things, like help with homework and how to cook beans on toast. How to talk to girls and reading the stories boys liked before bed. Things he'd get from a father who lived in the *same* house.

Then he almost staggered as an unbearable thought slammed into him. What if Beth remarried? What if another man lived with Marco day in, day out? What if—he flinched as if protecting himself from an incoming blow—another man lay in Beth's bed at night, held her in his arms, lost himself inside her.

He stopped abruptly and, hands low on his hips, faced her where she stood a few paces behind. "Tell me what it'll take to change your mind about marriage."

She stared off into the distance to the misty blue snowcapped mountains for a long moment before turning to him, her expression impossible to read. "Why do you want to marry me?"

"For Marco," he said without hesitation. "It's the best thing for him."

"Is there no other reason?" she pressed.

"What reason could there possibly be?" Even as he asked the question, a vision of her writhing under him only hours earlier filled his senses.

She took a step closer and looked up at him, a hint of a challenge in her eyes. "Is there any chance for us?"

Muscles taut, Nico gripped the wire lines the vines had been trained on and hissed out a breath through his teeth. How could she ask that of him? Had she any idea of what she'd really done in her efforts to keep her sordid secrets hidden? What she'd cost him?

"If we tried," she continued, not backing down from his reaction, "do you think it could become a real marriage in time?"

He coughed out a cynical laugh and twisted away. "I suppose that depends on your definition of a real marriage."

A group of quail landed a little way off and began to scratch in the dry dirt. He gazed at the little birds before realizing Beth had been quiet too long. He turned back and she met his gaze and held it before replying. "You know what my definition of marriage is, Nico."

He turned away again to hide his grimace as the memory hit. The two of them lying on a blanket on the edge of his home vineyard, an overflowing picnic basket beside them, sharing their hopes and dreams for the future. Their amazement at the similarity of their visions for a perfect marriage—deep love, fiery passion, tender affection and unconditional trust.

He'd been such a fool back then. So damn *young* and

wanting to believe he could have it all. He may as well have believed in the tooth fairy.

He walked farther into the vineyard, wanting to be as far away from the memories she evoked as possible, though he was aware Beth followed. He paused to run his hand along a strong pinot noir vine; they'd always been his favorite. Vines, grapes and wine had been constants in his life.

More than he could say for the woman walking behind him. She'd blown into his life when they were younger, turned it upside down, then left. And here she was again, this time making requests of him she had no right to make.

If we tried, do you think it could become a real marriage in time?

He set his shoulders and faced her. "We'll share Marco, a house and a bed." It was all he could offer. All he had inside him to offer anyone.

"Marco, a house and a bed," she repeated slowly, her blue eyes glistening.

Her unguarded emotion struck him deep in the gut but he fought against it, narrowing his eyes. "Do you dare ask for more?"

"I won't settle for less than a real partnership if I marry again, Nico." She drew in a shaky breath. "But we can't ever have that, can we?"

"No." He bit the word out, definite and angry before stalking off down between rows of waist-high vines. His movements startled a falcon, which rose on its powerful wings and hovered close by.

This examination of his heart, this expectation that

he'd open it again, was intolerable. He'd spent five years with his heart buried under layer upon layer of protective shields and here Beth was, wanting to rip them away for no purpose.

He heard her stop behind him as he inspected a cane that would soon bud with new growth.

"They say time heals all wounds," she said softly from behind him.

Incredulous, he pivoted to face her. He'd *never* forget her abandoning him with no word of warning or explanation. Could never forgive her taking his son to protect her shady past. "Some things are beyond the concept of healing."

She nodded slowly. "You'll never trust me."

"How could I after what you've done?" he demanded.

"I suppose I can't expect anything more than that. But I won't marry under those conditions, Nico." She swallowed hard and took a small step back. "I'd hoped that one day you could forgive me. That maybe, based on what we'd once shared, you could find forgiveness in your heart."

Nico ground his teeth together. Yes, he'd once thought they'd shared something special. Thought *she* was special. Different from the social climbers and false women who'd always surrounded him.

But she'd shown her true colors eventually. Deep down, she'd been no different. She'd earnestly vowed nothing would ever keep her from him, then left the country with his brother at the first test of that promise.

"Okay," he said, tightly leashing his emotions, "let's talk about trust. *You* trust *me* and tell me what Kent was blackmailing you with."

Her bottom lip trembled. "I can't."

"So you say." He arched an eyebrow; she'd proved his point. "You didn't trust me with it then, you won't trust me with it now."

Beth's eyes implored him for sympathy, but she'd lost the right to his sympathy the day she'd first hidden his son. Stolen those irreplaceable years, days, minutes, moments.

She rubbed her hands up and down her arms as if suddenly chilled. "Nico, it's—"

"Although," he cut her off, unwilling to listen to more excuses, "I suppose I should thank you for one thing. Before I met you I was too naive by a long mile." He shook his head at his own stupidity. "I believed in magical ideas of love, of faithfulness, of loyalty. But I learnt the lesson well. Never put your heart on the table for someone to pulverize. *Never trust anyone.*"

He'd lived his life by that creed since she'd left and he wasn't about to change philosophies now—especially not for the woman who'd taught him the lesson in the first place.

It was over. Really over.

No matter the want, the need she still had for him deep in her bones, there was no going back to what they'd once shared. Beth stared at the back of Nico's head as he walked purposefully back the way they'd come.

Her insides torn apart by the realization, she followed him.

Though, in all honesty, it'd been over since the night five years ago when she'd left him with no explanation. The only possible hope after that had been a stubborn figment of her imagination. She'd hung on to visions of him, of him loving her, almost believing it somehow connected them—that he would feel it, too. But all he felt was betrayal…and the connection to Marco.

When she reached the playground, Nico already stood waiting for her beside his Alfa Romeo. Would this be the last time they traveled in a car together? The last time they would be within touching distance? She knew he worried about having enough participation in Marco's life, that he didn't trust her, but she would do everything in her power to make sure Marco and Nico had unrestricted access to each other—a father–son relationship was too important for anything less. But sharing Marco didn't mean she and Nico need have any contact. It could all be done through lawyers and go-betweens.

At the thought of it, though she would have sworn ten minutes ago it wasn't possible, her heart broke a little more.

He held her passenger door open while she slid in—chivalrous despite being angry. But part of her couldn't blame him for that. His bitterness was the result of her own actions—hers and Kent's.

"Nico," she ventured once he was in the driver's seat. "Have you been this angry the whole time we've been apart?"

Expression stony, he turned the key and the sports car roared to life. Then his heavy-lidded eyes cast her a withering glance. "I've been having the time of my life since you left. Or don't you read the papers?"

Oh, yes, she'd seen the stories of wild three-day parties, of him dropping large sums of cash in casinos and flipping speedboats on the French Riviera.

"That man in the media coverage isn't the same man I knew." The man she'd loved more than her own life. "You've changed. And it pierces my soul to think of you staying this way forever...." This parody of the loving, giving man he'd been, with such a passion for life.

"Fact of life—everyone changes. I apologize if my changes don't meet with your approval." The sarcasm in his voice was heavy and biting.

She pulled the sunglasses from her head to shade her eyes from the early afternoon sun as the car sped along the country road. "Nothing remains of what we once had, does it? Even our memories are tainted. We have no past left, no present, no future."

He gave a humorless laugh. "That's an understatement. Marco will always connect us, but I see no reason why we need to have any role in each other's life."

His bitterness slammed into her anew and she bit down on her bottom lip to stop it from trembling. She might not have felt she had a choice at twenty, but she'd still been the one who'd triggered this change in Nico.

Sorry would never be enough. After the love he'd so freely given her when they were younger, she owed him more. Owed him what healing she could offer.

But what could she do? A woman he didn't want to see

again? He'd once told her that she was his world. That as long as she was by his side, he needed nothing more. When he'd said that, she'd felt as if she were standing on the top of a mountain, as if she were invincible. His love had been her air. His companionship, her nectar. His body, her banquet.

She gripped the seat belt that crossed her body. "Do you think we'll ever love anyone else," she whispered hoarsely, "the way we did before all this started?"

His mouth opened, and the scorn in his eyes told her another rebuke was coming. But then he closed it again. Swallowed hard. "No," he rasped. "It's never been with anyone the way it was with you."

That little window into his heart made her breath catch in her throat. She still had a chance to reach him.

She had no doubt now—it was her responsibility to help him heal. To help him bring out his tenderness again. Marco would need it from him, and Nico needed it himself, whether he realized it or not.

Their lovemaking had once been passionate, yet so beautifully tender—the antithesis of last night, which had been as much about regaining what he'd lost as it was about passion; and so much more than what they'd shared this morning in her bedroom.

Perhaps she could reach him by making beautiful love, the way they had five years ago, with all her heart and soul, no barriers, no self-protection. Somewhere, deep down, Nico would surely respond to that, to her. No guarantees, she knew, but it was the only plan she had—heal him with her love for both his and Marco's sake.

Nico pulled into her driveway, and when he reached the parking area at the front of her house, left the engine idling.

Despite her heart beating wildly, Beth mustered all her courage. It was now or never.

Now, her body whispered, reawakened by the thought of having one last chance to lay down with him. Of him touching her skin a final time, of touching his, of losing herself in him.

"Would you like to come in?" she asked in a voice that only slightly wavered.

Nico frowned. She'd surprised him—a good start. And she'd need to keep one step ahead of him if her plan was to work.

He ran a frustrated hand through his hair. "What would be the point? We're at an impasse."

"I'd like to give you some photos of Marco. For the years you've…you've missed." A peace offering. And once she had him inside, she could begin to make it up to him properly. To make love to him with no safety net, to help him heal and become the real Nico again.

He considered for a moment, then, his face expressionless, nudged the gear stick into place and cut the engine. With her nerves clamoring for an outlet, Beth jumped out and almost ran to the door. She fumbled with the key in the lock, then stopped, closed her eyes and took a deep breath. Nerves were counterproductive, she'd stumble and say the wrong thing, do the wrong thing. If she was to pull this off, she had to be calm and centered.

Knowing Nico stood behind her—so close, yet so far—she turned the key and led the way in. The warmth from the central heating meant she could discard her coat on the hook beside the door, but Nico kept his on—he obviously wasn't planning to stay long. She'd change that soon enough. She had to.

Beth walked to the cabinet where she'd hidden the photos yesterday and retrieved several—the ones she'd want to see if she were in his shoes: Marco standing proud with his first swimming certificate, sitting on Santa's knee when he was three, surrounded by presents on his second birthday, and the earliest photo she had of him taken in hospital the day he was born. She bit down on her lip, filled with emotion for her beloved child. She was doing this for him, too; he needed a father with an intact heart.

She would give Marco's father all she had to give, for all their sakes. And hope it was enough to repair five years' worth of damage to his heart….

She handed the frames to Nico with a trembling hand. He took them then stepped away, making a quarter turn to face the mantle—away from her. Beth wrapped her arms around herself, pointlessly wishing this had been an experience they could share together. But Nico needed breathing space if she had any hope of reaching him.

Taking his time, he looked at each snapshot one by one. As he paused on the second one, his throat worked up and down; on the third, he murmured words in Italian. When he reached the last one, the picture of Marco as a newborn, he traced his finger over the glass, blinking rapidly. "So tiny," he whispered as if to himself.

Tears stinging her eyes, Beth pressed a hand to her mouth, holding back the emotion, trying not to disturb Nico's privacy.

He looked up and caught her watching, his eyes filled with warmth in this unguarded moment. "Thank you. I didn't expect…" He cleared his throat. "After what I said in the car…" He shook his head and looked back at the pictures of their son.

A seed of joy took root in her chest. She'd touched his heart. She could see him, see a shadow of *Nico,* the man she'd fallen so deeply in love with.

She smiled, soft and open. "You're welcome. You deserve them—and more."

He didn't reply but his forehead creased as if processing her words. It was time to take it the extra step. They had no future—he'd confirmed it himself earlier—but she'd help him to find his tenderness again.

"By the way," she said evenly. "I don't believe this facade of a hard-hearted rogue you've been showing the world—and me."

He looked up sharply, an eyebrow raised and waited.

She took a small step closer. "You have a heart the size of Australia and you'll never hide it completely. You're a good man, Nico Jordan."

His eyes bored into hers, all traces of his earlier, more sensitive emotions gone. "You don't know me anymore."

One corner of his mouth curved in a mocking smile. "If you've followed the papers at all in the last few years, you'd know I'm a scoundrel who doesn't deserve anyone's faith."

Those stories weren't about the real him, the true heart of Nico. She looked up at him through her lashes as she moved another step closer. So close she could feel his body warmth. "Well, you have my faith, whether you think you deserve it or not."

He took a step back, looking cold and challenging— yet his eyes had gone dark and somehow wary. "You're trying to change my mind. Convince me I'm a good person so I won't demand marriage for Marco's sake." He crossed his arms. "It won't work."

She didn't deny it, he wouldn't understand yet anyway. Instead, she reclaimed the step he'd taken and laid a hand on his strong forearm. "I believe in you."

And she took the last step and kissed him with all her faith, all her belief—all her love. His lips were hard and unyielding, but she didn't falter, moving her hands up to slide through his thick, wavy hair. She kissed his top lip, his lower lip, *showing* him what he wouldn't accept in words.

"No," he said, but it was more of a groan, a plea, than a command—and for one sweet moment, he kissed her back, hungrily, as he uncrossed his arms and gripped her elbows. Then he stopped.

He pulled away, eyes closed and frowning, as if in pain. "Beth," he rasped. "I don't know what you think you're doing, but it won't change a thing."

She swayed against him. "I'm not trying to change

things between us. You'll go your way and I'll go mine and we'll both be parents to Marco. But right now, in this moment, I'm touching you because I want to." She feathered a kiss on the strong line of his jaw. "*Need* to."

She raised a hand and laid it over his heart, feeling it race. "Tell me you don't want to kiss me," she challenged huskily.

"You know I want to, that's never been in question." He lifted his gaze to the ceiling, as if trying to compose himself, but unwittingly giving her access to his strong throat, lightly bristled in the afternoon light. She kissed it, relishing the heat of his skin against her lips.

"Then do it, Nico." She scraped her teeth along the side of his neck. "Kiss me."

His body shuddered and finally he gave in. He cradled her head in his hands and gently pressed his lips to hers, holding her there, as if savoring the feel. Her limbs all but melted. She'd dreamed of this so often—of a *real* kiss with him—that part of her wondered if it was truly happening. But his musky scent surrounded her, and the masculine perfection of his mouth was too real to be a dream.

Her fingers curled and unfurled against his chest, lost in the simple act of giving and taking. Of sharing.

He splayed one hand over her bottom and pressed her against him, perhaps to show that she played with fire, but the feel of his erection roused her craving further and she shifted her hips against him.

Memories of pleasing him flooded her mind, of

spending glorious hours exploring his body and his reactions. She wanted it all again, this one last time.

She unbuttoned his shirt, slowly, without breaking the kiss, then let the sides fall apart to bare his bronze chest to her seeking fingers. His skin was warm under her fingertips, his chest hair coarse, and as she brushed his flat nipple, he made a low sound in his throat.

They fit together, matched. Were made for each other. How would she ever let him go after this? She blocked the thought before it took root. She'd worry about that later. For now she only wanted this time together. For both of them.

His hands dropped to her waist as he kissed down the column of her throat. She let her neck arch back, reveling in the beauty of the sensation. His lips—so gentle, so masterful—trailed heat and delicate biting kisses along her skin.

This was the Nico she remembered, the Nico she'd hoped to reach.

She pressed a moist kiss to his bare shoulder, the male scent of his naked skin filling her senses, and his grip on her waist tightened a little. As her body thrummed to beautiful life, she ran her lips across his smooth shoulder. When she reached the strong muscles of his neck, no other sound registered in her brain besides his breathing, heavy with want. Thoughts of making love to heal his heart faded, pushed to the background by the intensity of desire.

"Bella," he rasped, then delicious heat licked her veins as his hands moved down to curve around her hips.

With a groan, he pulled back and looked deep into her eyes. His pupils were dilated with desire, his breathing ragged, but he moved with exquisite patience to smooth her hair back from her face. "God, I've missed you."

She hitched in a breath. "I thought I'd die without you," she whispered.

Nico felt the honesty of her words deep in his heart, and at that moment, the jagged ice that had lived there for five long years shattered into splinters and began to melt.

He enfolded her in his arms, bringing her body close, shaping her curves to him. He'd thought it was too late, that his heart and soul were long dead, but she was reawakening that part of him. No, it'd started with his first glimpse of Marco in the park today—probably why he'd tried so hard to cling to his son—but now this miracle of a woman was bringing his soul roaring back to life.

She melded against him for a several beats, holding him tightly, then she laid a palm on his chest and pressed until she had enough room to push his shirt down past his wrists and onto the floor. Her gaze caressed him in a way no other woman's ever had—she saw him, really saw him, not just his name or money—and it sent a rush of tenderness through his system.

Returning the favor, he flicked the buttonholes of her blouse with quick motions. When it fell apart, his fingers traced the lilac lace of her bra with reverence. Such beauty. She'd always been so perfect to him that she'd been almost elusive, a little piece of heaven in his arms. He cupped her breast, feeling the light pressure of her taut nipple against his palm. Her murmurs of encouragement gave his hands a life of their own, and they gently pulled the lace down, allowing him to dip his head and taste the delicate skin.

His teeth nipped lightly on the soft, creamy side of her breast—she tasted like strawberries. Sweet. Intoxicating.

Her hands stroked his back in an urgent caress, fueling the hum of pent-up need that pervaded every cell of his body. In all their time apart, even knowing of her betrayal, his body had never stopped wanting her in his arms like this.

He lifted his head, seeking her succulent lips and claiming them once more while his hand slid between their bodies and slowly unzipped her trousers until they fell to the floor. He stroked the pad of his thumb over her lace and satin panties and she moaned into his mouth.

His hands slipped beneath her panties then around to lovingly cradle her bottom. He pushed the panties aside, needing to touch her warm lushness, exultant when the rhythm of her breaths became more urgent.

In a haze of passion, he swung her into his arms and carried her across the room to her large, overstuffed couch.

"Nico," she said huskily.

He paused midstride, looking down at her with her blouse hanging open and her trousers gone, revealing her lilac bra and panties and his breath caught.

"No woman alive…" he whispered as he leaned down to snatch a kiss "…as beautiful as you."

He carried her to the couch and laid her down,

reverentially. Quickly discarding the rest of his clothes and donning protection from his wallet, he stretched out beside her, eyes drawn to the fluttering pulse at her throat. He kissed it, licked the spot that showed just how close she was to losing control.

As she reached to stroke his chest, his shoulders, his arms, her bra strained to confine her breasts. He released the clasp and freed them for his hands. So soft as they filled his palms, so smooth under his fingertips.

Pushing her panties down her legs, he felt almost light-headed at the sight of her body now completely revealed to him. He raked his hands down her sides, watching the rise and fall of her breasts, knowing there had never been a more perfect moment since the beginning of time.

"Nico," she gasped, "I need you inside me."

He could deny her nothing. Lifting himself on his arms, he rose over her, knelt between her thighs, marveling that she was here once more, open to him, wanting him. He lowered himself over her to kiss her flushed face and tenderly plunder her mouth. Then, with a measured rock of his hips, he entered her, worshiping her with his body.

She reached to stroke his back, his shoulders, his chest, and his hypersensitive skin felt the touch like sparks of electricity.

He felt the build of tension in her body, rode her harder, reached between them to the place where they joined. Her body arched convulsively before she quivered and shattered in his arms, gasping, screaming his name.

Then his mind blanked with the roar of his release and all he knew was Beth. Beth under him. Beth enveloping him. Beth.

And only one thought penetrated—leaving her wasn't an option.

Nine

Nico drove into the winery car park an hour later, cut the engine and leaned his head back on the headrest. It'd damn near killed him to leave Beth's bed. After making love to her he'd watched her fall asleep, the mid-afternoon light filtering through her windows illuminating her face. She'd looked like an angel.

He couldn't join her in sleep, however, he had things to do before leaving tomorrow morning. He'd be back very soon, but today he'd wanted to buy his son a present and he'd promised his father he'd find Kent's copy of the Deed of Gift.

Once he had the deed, he was returning to Beth, slipping back between her cotton sheets and not leaving until his flight for anything short of an earthquake. His pulse picked up speed and he smiled. He'd be back as soon as he sorted a few details in Australia.

He snapped off his seat belt and jumped out, keen to get this task over with as quickly as possible. Andrew, the acting winemaker was waiting for him just inside the entrance and escorted him down a stone-tiled corridor to Kent's office.

Being in the winery again filled him with delicious memories of Beth on the terrace at the launch. The launch had been less than twenty-four hours ago; he couldn't believe how much had changed since then. That stolen kiss in the darkness had been heart-stopping, but it was nothing compared to the kisses they would share from now on. They would be together.

Marco needed both his parents together. He would convince Beth one way or another.

"Here we are, Mr. Jordan," Andrew said as he unlocked a door with Kent's name on a brass panel.

Nico stepped into his brother's office and grimaced. The room reeked of spite and malice. Or maybe that said more about his feelings for Kent than the office itself.

Even as children, he and Kent had never shared anything resembling brotherly love, and now Kent was dead, Nico still couldn't summon any grief that his half brother was gone. Reality was, his brother had hated him and done everything in his power to hurt him. Including blackmailing away the woman Nico once loved.

His gut began to constrict and twist the way it always did when he thought of how Kent had gloated over "paying" Beth to abandon him. He clenched his fists and looked around Kent's workspace. He didn't want to be in this damn office, touching his brother's things, remembering scenes best locked away.

Reeling himself in, he unclenched his hands and turned to the acting winemaker. "Thank you, Andrew. I appreciate you coming down on a Sunday to let me in."

Andrew smiled easily. "You're welcome, Mr. Jordan. Anything else I can do?"

How about telling me where Kent hid his copy of the Deed of Gift so I can get the hell out of here?

But Nico shook his head. "I can take it from here."

Andrew handed over the key chain. "I'll leave you Mr. Jordan's set of keys. When you're done, you can leave them with Barb in the shop."

Nico nodded his assent and watched Andrew leave before dropping into the executive chair and glancing around the office his brother had worked from for the past five years.

Since the day Kent had stolen Beth from him.

The coil of hatred for his brother rose again, but it was tempered by the vision of Beth, waiting for him, warm and soft in her bed. His blood turned to pure liquid heat, knowing he'd join her as soon as he found the deed. He looked around the room, searching for places Kent would have kept papers.

A squirming at his chest reminded him of the present he'd bought Marco on the way. He unzipped his bomber jacket to see Oliver's small black head snuggled against his shirt, the puppy's weight supported by the jacket's waistband. "Hey, little guy."

The ten-week-old puppy opened sleepy eyes and

looked up at him and Nico scratched the top of his head with a finger. He'd looked at about thirty dogs before he'd seen a sweet black puppy with huge feet and a soft head, and once he'd picked him up, Nico had known he was the one for Marco. The shelter thought he was a Labrador cross and said they were a great breed for kids.

He ran a finger along one of Oliver's velvet ears. "Just give me a few minutes to go through some things here and I'll take you to your new house."

Oliver yawned and curled up again, so Nico zipped his bomber jacket higher and started sorting through papers on Kent's desk.

Andrew had been in here, acting in Kent's position, so the most immediate needs of the winery had been taken care of, but there was a deed that Nico, Kent and their father had all signed about the future handover of Jordan Wines stock that Nico wanted. When a Jordan Wines lawyer had contacted Beth and Andrew, neither had been able to find the document. The lawyers said finding all copies of the contract wasn't necessary because the new Deed of Gift that Tim had instructed be written to outline the stock handover to Nico and Marco would supercede it, but Tim was a stickler for order and wanted all three copies before writing up the new deed.

Nico glanced around. When Kent had worked for Jordan Wines in Australia, he'd always had a secret compartment in his desk. Nico had been fourteen and training under his father after school and on holidays when he'd first discovered Kent's habit. His father would occasionally send him to assist Kent on matters, and

Kent would naturally take the opportunity to belittle and humiliate his younger half brother. Nico would never tell their father, but there was one thing he could do as a fourteen-year-old to even the scales.

He would find the key to Kent's secret compartment— or find the new compartment when Kent built an additional one—and leave the contents on the desk for Kent to find when he returned. A stupid child's prank that would have done no more than annoy his brother, but it had given Nico some satisfaction at the time.

He felt now under the desk, looking for an extra compartment that couldn't be easily seen. Bingo. Off to the right, where the one in his second Australian desk had been located. Crouching, he felt the front of the drawer with his fingers until he found a keyhole. Nico checked the key chain Andrew had left and sure enough, there was a small key that should fit. He tried it, and the lock released.

Kent hadn't gone to much trouble to hide the key— though without a mischievous teenage brother hanging around, he probably hadn't needed to. Nico pulled open the drawer and reached in. It was full of papers, so he drew the lot out and placed them on the desktop.

He flicked through bank statements from an account Beth probably didn't know about, and receipts from places Nico didn't want to know about, finding nothing. One long, sealed envelope looked aged and was blank on the front, so he slit the top open and pulled out the pages. Handwritten notes on yellowed paper; not the deed about the stock handover. About to toss them back, the name at the top caught his attention.

Adelina. His mother.

Frowning, he read the unfamiliar scrawl.

My dearest Adelina,

You tear at my soul! You say you must stay with your husband, that you love him, that it was just one night between us, but don't you understand I love you? I've never loved anyone the way I love you. Please, please don't end this, my darling.

How could you say it was a mistake, that we had nothing between us, when we made a baby from our love? You and I and little Nico could be a family if—

Lungs frozen, unable to read more, Nico dropped down into the chair, his knees no longer prepared to carry his weight. He turned the note over, desperately hoping to see his father's name at the end, but knowing in his gut it wouldn't be.

Yours forever,

James.

Nausea swirled in his stomach, sweat broke out across his forehead. His mother had cheated. Tim Jordan, the man who'd raised him and loved him, wasn't his father.

He tried to picture his mother involved in this subterfuge, but the suggestion was implausible.

Or was it?

A small kernel of doubt squirmed in his chest. His

mother had always been unconventional. The daughter of an Italian count, she'd been brought up to believe she was above the rules made for other people. She'd lived her life large and filled with passion. Could she…

No. That was a step too far. She'd loved both him and his father more than life. She'd never have betrayed either of them. It was a lie fabricated by either Kent or Lois, his mother, or both.

Even as he had the thought, snatches of memory surfaced to taunt him…. Lying in a hospital bed at eleven years old, his mother furtively talking to the doctors when giving his medical history…. His mother's blush when he'd exclaimed as a fourteen-year-old that in biology lessons he'd calculated how he'd inherited hair, eye and skin color from her, with nothing from his father….

His fists curled into a clench so tight, his knuckles hurt. It was true, he had to acknowledge it. He was illegitimate. He'd loved Tim as much as any son could love a father, but it was based on a lie.

How could his mother have kept this from him? From his father? Nico paced across the room, trying to bring order to his tumbling thoughts. What of this… James? He'd given up on his biological son because of a rejection from a woman—or had more gone on there?

And Kent had known! Nico stopped pacing and pinched the bridge of his nose. The situation suddenly felt even grubbier than it had a moment ago.

Although, this didn't make sense—why wouldn't Kent proclaim Nico's illegitimacy to the world…?

And then it *did* make sense. *This is what Kent had*

used to blackmail Beth. He swore, using every unsavory oath he could think of.

She'd left him in some misguided attempt to protect him!

He let his head sink into his hands. What mess had she created? Instead of coming to him, sharing this with him, Beth had run away, taking with her any chance Nico would have of talking to his mother before she died. Beth had cheated him almost as much as his mother and Kent had, damn it.

Nico took a deep, slow breath, bringing himself back under control. He needed to call his father, give him the chance to rewrite his will before it was too late. That was only fair.

Besides, if three people—that he knew of—had heard about the letters, there was a chance it would make its way back to his father on its own. Nico's gut clenched at the thought. His father had been knocked hard by Kent's death, especially with the virtual estrangement that had existed. And Tim Jordan was more than family; he was someone Nico loved and respected. Someone he'd protect with his life.

If his father had to hear a malicious rumor, it was best it came from him. He grabbed his cell phone from his pocket and dialed his father's number in Australia.

His father picked up on the third ring. "Hello?"

"Dad, it's Nico." Calling him Dad felt good, felt right, as if affirming their relationship even if no biological link existed.

"How's it going over there?" The smile in his father's voice was clear through the international phone line.

"Fine. I'll call you later with a report. But there's something I have to tell you now."

"You'd better go ahead then." His father's voice became serious, obviously picking up on the tension in his own.

"I've found some papers among Kent's things." His voice was tight as he struggled to control himself under the onslaught of the day.

There was a long pause. "I think you'd better tell me what this is about."

"There were letters about you and me. Look, you need to know this but swear to me that you won't get worked up."

"Son, just tell me what they said." He didn't sound as worried as Nico had expected, which was good news, if curious.

"They say—" he dragged in a lungful of air "—that you're not my father."

A resigned oath came down the line before Tim said simply, "Son, I know."

Nico felt an electric bolt of shock hit every cell in his body. *"What?"* Had he misheard?

"You're not my biological son, but don't you for a *second* believe I'm not your father." Tim's voice was fierce with love. "I've raised you and I love you as much as any father could. You're mine."

Nico felt as if the room was doing a slow spin around him but he gathered himself and forced his voice to work. "How long have you known?"

Tim's sigh was full of reluctance. "Since your mother was pregnant. She never knew that I found out—I couldn't risk losing her, so I kept her secret. And once I saw you, held you, I loved you as much as if you shared my blood, and I couldn't risk losing you, either. Your mother went to her grave thinking our family unit was safe, and she was right."

Nico's world had shrunk to the phone at his ear, to this bizarre conversation. "So who was he, this James?" He forced the words out through a jaw that had seized tight.

"I have some information in a folder that I've kept in case you ever needed it. I'll have it ready for when you get back."

This couldn't be happening. It was too much to comprehend. Not only was he illegitimate, but his father had known all his life.

"I'll understand if you want to change your will."

"Why would I want to do that? You're my son, biology be damned. And there's no man on this Earth I'd rather have for a son. You make me proud every day."

A lump of emotion filled his throat. "Thanks," Nico said, voice rough.

"It's no more than the truth. When are you coming home?"

"Soon, Dad. Soon. I have some things to do first." He gripped the letters until they crumpled. He needed to speak to Beth about the secrets in these pages that she'd hidden from him—to ask how she could possibly justify it.

"Have you been able to see little Mark?" His father's words were full of hope.

"Yes." Nico smiled and closed his eyes, picturing

Marco's face as he plunged down the slide and into his arms. "And it seems I'm not the only one with a paternity surprise."

He could hear muffled noises, as if his father was moving the phone to his other ear. "What do you mean?"

"He's not Kent's son. He's mine." Nico felt his chest expand a little as he announced the news to someone for the first time.

"You're joking," Tim said, sounding as shell-shocked as Nico had been when he'd realized.

"There's no question. I'll be home tomorrow and I'll explain everything then—it's a long story." A story centering around a woman with red-gold hair and a remarkable capacity for keeping secrets. Nico reined in his anger and focused back on his father. "I'll have photos of your grandson with me and I'll organize to bring him for a visit soon."

"I'd like that. Talk when you get back."

Nico disconnected the phone and slipped it back into his pocket with shaking fingers.

His father had known.

Everyone had known about his paternity but him.

He rubbed his throbbing temples. He could understand his father's fear of losing him, and his mother's fear of losing them both. And he could understand Kent wanting to use the information for the most personal advantage.

But the *one* person he should have been able to trust to tell him something this important, the one person who should have been playing on his team, was the woman he'd loved. The woman he'd wanted to marry and form an unbreakable partnership with. His heart hammered like it was going to beat right out of his chest.

But Beth had obviously had different ideas about what constituted a partnership, because she sure as hell hadn't treated him like a partner the day she'd made a decision for him and left.

Ten

Beth woke alone, shivering. No man beside her or sounds from the shower. She'd been waking alone for the better part of five years—besides the nights Marco crawled into her bed—but never before had it seemed so empty. So cold. So *wrong*.

She squinted at her bedside clock—4:00 p.m. She must have slept for less than an hour.

Grabbing a gown, she padded around her room, tying the sash at her waist as she went. "Nico?"

No answer. Could he have left? She lifted the blinds to check the front of the house. His car was gone.

Her stomach dropped so fast she felt a little dizzy. It hadn't worked then, the plan to bring out his tenderness. Once again he'd ravished her body then abandoned her.

She rested her head on the oiled-wood windowsill, hopelessness washing through every cell of her body. Perhaps she'd been wrong all those years ago. Perhaps she should have just told Nico about the letters and let him choose his course from there. But, whatever the answer, it was too late for regrets or what ifs. She couldn't go back, and she couldn't undo the damage.

Just before she dropped the blind, movement caught her attention—her parents' car coming down the driveway. Her heart lifted as if on wings. Marco's big, welcoming smile as he pressed his face to the car window was exactly what she needed right now. A distraction from her thoughts, but even more importantly, just to see her son again.

She quickly threw on a dress, ran a brush through her hair and rushed to greet them.

When she opened the door, all three were there stamping their feet on the wire mat, faces rosy from the cool afternoon air, and before any of them had a chance to say a word of greeting, she lifted Marco and held him tightly to her chest. She needed the affirmation of love and life that hugging his small body always brought.

Marco squirmed at the constricting embrace and, with a final kiss on the top of his dark hair, she reluctantly let him go.

Her father caught her in a bear hug. "Hello, sweetheart," he said over her head.

"Hi, Dad." She let herself relax into the hug, and was a little disappointed when he ended it and unknowingly withdrew the comfort she craved right now.

She stepped away and greeted her mother who

searched her eyes before asking, "Darling, is everything okay?"

Beth's mind drifted to Nico. To the kisses he'd so gently placed on her cheeks, her eyelids, her lips… To his absence without a word of goodbye…

She covered her mouth with her hand in case she betrayed her grief and took a step back. She owed her parents some sort of explanation of the weekend's events, but she wouldn't say a word against anyone involved while Nico's son could hear.

She pointedly glanced at Marco then back to her mother. "Everything's good."

Her mother pursed her lips, understanding. "Perhaps we could have a talk later?"

Arduous though that would be, Beth gave a quick nod. It had to happen eventually, and the sooner the better.

They moved into the kitchen and Beth began the familiar and comforting ritual of making coffee and hot chocolate. Marco scrambled up on a stool, directly across the bench from her.

"Mummy, was that man today really my uncle?" His face held no suspicion; his eyes were bright with curiosity and eagerness.

Her breath caught. It was the perfect opening, if sooner than she'd hoped. Despite what had happened between her and Nico, he still deserved a relationship with his son. And Marco had a right to it. It was her job to lay down the foundations now, as she'd promised Nico earlier. Allow Nico to claim Marco as his own child.

Drawing in a measured lungful of air, she turned to

her parents with an apologetic palm raised. "Mum, Dad, could we have a few minutes, please?"

Her parents nodded and left quietly. She heard them turning the television on in the next room, giving her the privacy she needed for Marco's sake as well as her own.

Beth put down the mug she held in her hand and leaned over the bench so she was eye to eye with her son. "Sweetie, he's a little more than that."

Marco frowned, thinking it through. "Like a special uncle?"

Beth smiled, reassuring her precious child as she tested the waters. "Would you like him to be?"

Marco nodded emphatically. "He was nice. He's gonna buy me a dog!"

Beth blinked rapidly, holding the tears at bay. *Marco liked him.* Though she hadn't really doubted it after watching them play on the slide, and Marco's glances of hero worship.

The reality hit again. Marco would have loved his father, and she'd denied them *both* these four years. But she pushed the thought and the guilt away. She was about to throw her son the biggest curve ball of his short life and she needed all her focus on doing it right.

She walked around the bench and sat on the stool beside him, holding her son's small hands in hers. "Yes, he is nice. But he's even more than a special uncle."

Marco hesitated, as if trying to solve the puzzle. "Then what is he?"

"Did you know that sometimes boys who are very lucky get to have two daddies?" Marco's eyes expanded as he took in the enormity of the revelation, but he didn't seem confused, so she continued. "And that man you met today is your other daddy."

A grin spread across her son's face, then he lurched forward and wrapped his arms tightly around her neck. She held him as close as she could, melting inside with love for her adorable little boy.

Marco whispered in her ear, "Mummy, I like this one."

Tears welled in her eyes and she let them fall unchecked, unwilling to release her brave son who'd been deprived of his true father until now through Kent's manipulations and her own imperfect notions of what was right for everyone.

Marco pulled back, joy still radiating in all his features. "When is my new daddy coming back?"

Her heart ached as she remembered Nico's desertion earlier, but she'd never been more sure of anything: he *would* be back. To see Marco.

"I'm not sure, sweetie. But remember he lives in Australia so he won't be here every night like your other daddy was." She stroked her thumb over his rosy cheek. "He has to go home in the morning, but he'll come and see you a lot."

Undeterred, Marco's eyes widened as another thought struck. "Can I call him Daddy?"

She bit down on her lip to hold back the smile, so pleased for both Nico and Marco's sake despite her own aching heart. "I think he'd like that."

His hands shot high in a victory pose, then just as

suddenly, dropped as his attention shifted. "Can I go play on my swing set?"

Beth looked to the window. It was still light but not for much longer. "Just for a little while, because it'll be dinnertime soon. And don't go out of the yard."

"Yes, Mum," he replied in a long-suffering voice.

She smiled and watched him collect his coat and gloves then run through the back door. She turned to look through the kitchen window to see him jump on his swing. Her precious son, her baby, was the most important thing in this whole mess with Nico and Kent. She wouldn't let anyone lose sight of that fact.

Her father's voice came from the doorway. "Now I think it's about time you told us what's going on here."

Beth looked from her father to her mother—the parents who'd followed her from Australia five years ago. Admittedly they were both retired and Beth was an only child, but it'd still been a huge move for them. She owed them the truth, even if it was a little late coming.

"Do you want a coffee?" She smiled uncertainly and looked to where she'd started making drinks before Marco's questions. "It's rather a long and complicated story."

And it wasn't over yet. Not when things were still in such a stalemate between her and Nico. When they had custody and visitation arrangements for Marco to settle.

A knock at the door startled her, made her pulse leap. Made her stupidly think of Nico, hoping it would be him, despite thinking only seconds earlier that things were in such a stalemate between them.

"Excuse me a moment," she said to her parents as she headed for the entranceway.

She opened the door and the air rushed from her lungs in one long whoosh. Nico stood as if conjured from her thoughts, wearing a bulky bomber jacket and casual jeans, his hair mussed into unruly rebel waves. And his face glowered like thunder incarnate. Was he angry she'd seduced him into her bed? Angry at himself for the tenderness he'd shown her?

She blinked and collected herself. "Hello, Nico."

"Hello, Beth." His sensual mouth curved in a parody of a smile, as if it amused him to observe the niceties when his mood was very obviously so black.

"We will talk soon," he said. "But first, I've brought Marco a present." He unzipped the front of his jacket to reveal a sleeping black bundle of fur.

At the sight of the darling thing, her heart melted. She couldn't hold herself back and reached out to stroke its velvet head. "A puppy."

With narrowed eyes, Nico watched her hand, less than an inch from his chest. "Oliver," he said curtly.

Her fingertips accidentally brushed the crisp fabric of his shirt and she saw his jaw clench a split second before he took a deliberate step back. She froze and the moment stretched. An icy breeze whipped past them, ruffling Nico's hair, the only movement as he stared her down.

She withdrew her hand and gripped the doorknob instead. Things had definitely changed between them.

Or perhaps nothing had changed—it was just she could no longer believe the illusion he could feel anything for her beyond bitterness.

She crossed her arms tight over her chest. "Marco's in the backyard. He'll be so excited."

He speared her with a heavy-lidded glance. "And after he's asleep, I have things to say."

"Yes." She stepped back, swallowed. They had a lot of arrangements to make regarding their son. Custody, visitation rights, financial arrangements, how they'd make decisions about Marco's life…it would be complex. "There's something you should know before you see him."

Nico's eyes blazed and swung in the direction of the backyard. "He's all right?"

"He's fine." Instinctively, she wanted to reach for his hand to reassure him, but he wouldn't thank her for the gesture. "I told him you're his father."

The blackness in his features dissolved and his voice was no more than a rasp. "How did he take it?"

She thought back to Marco gripping her neck in unrestrained joy. *Mummy, I like this one.* Her throat grew thick. "He took it exceptionally well. He said he liked you and asked if he could call you Daddy."

"He did?" The raw words barely carried to her ears.

She steeled herself and told him the second thing Marco had asked, the one that was hard to say aloud because it echoed her own deepest thoughts. "He wanted to know when you'd be back, but I didn't know what to tell him."

Nico stood impossibly taller. "Now he knows I'm his father, he'll be able to ask me questions directly."

Cutting out the middleman. Her. A spasm of pain ripped through her heart, but she beat it back and blinked to clear the thoughts. "You'd better come through so you can give Marco his present."

They walked through the house and Nico greeted her parents in the kitchen on the way. Her father smiled widely as he said hello, and she could see her mother's eyes crinkle in approval as she said his name. They'd been impressed watching Nico's interactions with Marco this afternoon. Beth was glad. He deserved the support of his son's grandparents.

When they stepped out the door, her sweet little boy looked up and came running, before stopping uncertainly in front of Nico. Her first impulse was to move in, reassure her son, smooth the interaction. But she needed to let them have this—to find their equilibrium. Besides, Nico would make sure Marco felt safe, she was sure of that.

Even as she had the thought, Nico smiled and crouched down. "Hello, Marco," he said gently. Welcomingly.

"Hello." Marco's smile spread tentatively across his face, but when it was full, it beamed. "Mummy says you're my other daddy."

Nico didn't flinch at the "other daddy" reference. She supposed she should have explained that to him at the door, but he handled it smoothly. "That's right. What do you think about that?"

"It's good," Marco said, as if he'd been handed the keys to his very own spaceship, and Beth's eyes filled with tears. "Mummy said I could call you Daddy. Is it really okay?"

Nico's Adam's apple worked up and down. "I'd like that a lot. Why don't you try it now?"

"Daddy." Marco glowed with happiness and threw himself at Nico, then pulled back in surprise, frowning at Nico's chest. "I think something moved in your coat."

A soft black head popped out from Nico's jacket, probably woken by the embrace, but was quick to take advantage. Oliver leaned forward and licked Marco's face in a long slurp, then whimpered to be released.

"A puppy." Marco's face lit up.

"*Your* puppy." Nico unzipped his jacket and tenderly put Oliver on the ground. "His name is Oliver."

Oliver waddled a few steps away and relieved himself then turned and ran to Marco, ears flapping, jumping up to rest his paws on his new favorite person's legs. Marco fell back on the grass, giggling.

"Thank you, Daddy," Marco said, looking up with Oliver on his chest.

Nico didn't answer right away, but when he did, his voice was rough. "You're welcome."

Beth felt herself breaking as she watched the scene of heartfelt emotion. Had she done the right thing in refusing Nico's proposal this afternoon? A tight band squeezed around her lungs and she struggled to draw breath. Despite the emotional torture it would inflict on them both, would it be better for their child if she and Nico married?

No, she had to believe she'd made the right choice. That a home full of tension and masked hostility would be detrimental to Marco—especially after the years living with Kent. Far better to have parents who loved him at two separate homes that were filled with joy and love. Her job now was to ensure the relationship between his parents looked like plain sailing so their son was never exposed to tension.

Marco jumped up and ran off. "Chase me, Oliver!" he called over his shoulder, and seeing fun afoot, the puppy followed as fast as his stubby legs would carry him.

She stepped closer to Nico. Time to begin that process of ensuring plain sailing. "You've done a very good thing. He'll never forget this day."

His eyes didn't leave Marco. "I wanted to give him something to remember me. To start to make up for the things he's missed," he said pointedly. "I'm going to make that my mission. From today, Marco will want for nothing from his father—materially or emotionally."

Her stomach hollowed when he said *To start to make up for the things he's missed* and she had to hold back the rush of guilt. It wouldn't achieve anything right now. They had to focus on the future. On keeping the channels between them smooth and tension-free.

She took a breath and redirected the conversation. "Where did you get Oliver? The shelter is closed Sundays."

He shrugged his strong shoulders, still not looking at her. "I offered them a sizable donation to open for me."

She smiled. Of course he had. "Creative of you."

He threw a sharp glance at her. "I wanted a dog for my son, so I bought a dog for my son."

Marco squealed as Oliver jumped all over him and Nico flashed a broad smile for his child.

Tears welled in her eyes as they watched Marco and Oliver run around in circles. It was almost everything she could want for her son. A father who was devoted to him, who would prioritize him. And yet a selfish corner of her heart whispered, *What about me, Nico? I want to be with you, too.* She loved him so much, needed him near her with an intensity that scared her, burned to have his trust again, his love. But her mind knew it was too late for them, too much water under the bridge. He'd stopped trusting her the day she'd left with Kent and never would again. She'd lost him.

She heard the door open behind them, saw her parents walk out to her side. Her mother nodded at Nico before turning to Beth. "Darling, you look like you have some... unfinished business. How about we take Mark and his new puppy home for the night? We'll drop them back tomorrow morning."

Beth's gaze slipped across to Nico. They did need time to discuss custody arrangements, perhaps holidays with Nico, new ways of making decisions about Marco's life. It was going to take a lot of negotiation and goodwill on both sides. She mentally crossed her fingers and hoped they had enough.

"Thank you, Mrs. Jackson," Nico answered for them both. "That's very considerate of you."

Her father clapped a hand on Nico's shoulder. "Least we can do. It seems you've had a big weekend."

A big weekend? A bubble of laughter threatened to escape her throat at the understatement. In forty-eight hours, Nico had discovered he had a son, met Marco and grappled with missing his first four years, found the only reason Beth had left him was blackmail, had his marriage proposal rejected and spoken at a wake for a brother who'd hated him.

She couldn't believe it was only yesterday morning that Nico had knocked on her door. So much had happened. So much had changed. So much had been lost.

No wonder Nico had seemed to be reeling for most of the weekend.

At least she'd been able to keep his illegitimacy—the most dangerous secret of all—from him, for now.

She turned to her mother. She'd only seen her son a few times in the two days, and she'd miss him like crazy if he went for another night, but it'd be best to have uninterrupted time to sort things without the concern that small ears were listening around the corner. "Thanks, Mum. Nico and I have some things to work out."

Marco came running over, closely followed by his new best friend and threw himself at Nico again, obviously thrilled to be able to hug his new daddy whenever he wanted. She suspected it would take a while for the novelty to wear off—for either father or son. Nico caught him and swung him up in the air.

Oliver whimpered to be so far below all the action and the hugging. Beth's father bent down to have a closer look. "And who is this little fellow?"

"That's Oliver," Marco piped up from Nico's arms. "He's mine."

Her father scooped up the tiny bundle of fur and held him in the crook of his arm. "Hello, Oliver. Nice to meet you. How would you and Mark like to come and stay at our house tonight so you can meet your new cousin Misty?"

Oliver licked the face talking to him.

Marco grinned. "Oliver says that's a good plan. Can we, Mum? Can I take Oliver to meet Misty?"

Beth leaned over to Marco, still being held by Nico, and kissed him on the cheek. "That sounds like a great idea."

"Yay! Misty will love him," Marco told Nico. "She'll want to play with us."

Her parents stepped toward the door. "Come on, let's get your pajamas," her mother said.

Nico hugged his son tightly and put him on the ground. "There are bowls, puppy food and a padded basket out beside my car."

Beth was grateful he'd thought ahead, but was sure the basket wouldn't be needed. If she guessed right, Oliver would spend every night on Marco's bed.

Her father stopped at the door and turned back to Nico, smiling. "We'll pack them in when we go out."

Beth watched her parents, Marco and Oliver all head for Marco's room, her stomach tightening. When they left, she and Nico would be alone. Once, she'd looked forward to those times with everything inside her, but that was a time long past. Now she wished she could delay the conversation that would formalize their new arrangement of separate lives. Lives that intersected only on the point of their son.

But that would only postpone the inevitable. She lifted her chin, ready to march to her fate and went inside to help her son pack.

Beth stood on her front porch, waving off her son and parents, Nico beside her. Tension radiated from him in waves—too much to just be about discussing arrangements for Marco. Her stomach fluttered. Was this about her seduction or was there more going on here?

Nico turned to her, his eyes fierce. "And now it's time for us to talk, *bella*."

Beth nodded, took a shaky breath and led the way into the living room. "Would you like a coffee?"

"No." His message in the one word was clear—he wanted to get this over with as soon as possible. He withdrew some folded papers from the back pocket of his jeans, flattened them and passed them to her, eyes trained on her face. "I found these hidden in Kent's office."

The room started to tip and slide as everything she'd built to protect Nico came crashing down around her ears. Even before they were in her hands, Beth recognized them: the letters Kent had produced the night he'd made his marriage demand. How she'd hated Kent in that moment, when he'd laid the ultimatum before her. Later she'd come to feel a blend of loathing and pity for her husband, but in that one instant she'd known she was capable of pure hatred.

She rolled the papers, gripped them in one hand and crossed her arms under her breasts, as if she could stop herself—and the world—from falling apart. "Where did you find them?"

"In a secret drawer. Kent always liked to hide things. Though, I guess he wasn't the only one," he said, his strong features accusing.

Oh, God above. She pressed together her lips hard in a futile attempt to hold back the emotion coursing through her body. After everything she'd sacrificed, Nico had learned the truth too soon and there wasn't a single thing she could do now. "I'm so sorry, Nico."

He waved away her words then pointed to her hand clutching the letters. "This is what Kent used to blackmail you with, isn't it?"

"Yes." As she said the word, she felt the last drop of light inside her evaporate, leaving her bereft. She'd been empty before—all these years with Kent—but she'd at least had the knowledge that she was protecting Nico and Tim to sustain her. Now even that was gone. She'd failed to protect the man she loved.

"So Kent showed you the letters and you left that night." He arched a sardonic eyebrow. "That was a bit rash—to not even think about it?"

"No," she said carefully, "I talked to someone before making the decision. Your mother." Her mind filled with the vision of Adelina on her parents' veranda, her dark eyes shining with tears of desperation. Nico's mother had confessed her mistake, declared that she would have done anything to change the past and make Nico Tim's true son.

"Do you love my Nico?" Adelina had asked Beth in her thick Italian accent.

"More than anything," Beth had replied.

"Then please don't tell him, I beg of you, it would hurt him too much. And if he never forgives me," she said as tears had slipped down her face, "he'd lose two parents at once."

Beth had vowed that she'd do whatever it took to ensure Nico didn't learn the truth.

Yet Adelina's plea to protect him from the information and Beth's sacrifice had come to nothing. The heart beating in her chest weighed almost more than she could bear.

His eyes flared. "And so now you bring my mother into your games when she can't defend herself. You could make up anything and tell me they were her words." His eyes glittered dangerously with betrayal and he stalked out the back door into the twilight.

Despite knowing this was virtually impossible for him to assimilate so soon and he'd need time, this final proof that he didn't trust her word still made her ache. But she had to put her pain behind. This was his pain, his suffering—the final betrayal. None of this was about her feelings.

She followed at a discreet distance, there if he needed her, not crowding him if he didn't. Her shoes were getting wet in the damp grass but she didn't care. She ached to hold him, to ease his torment, but she knew she had to give him some space. He reached Marco's swing set and raised an arm to lean against it, his shoulders and back tense.

She'd truly believed she was doing the right thing five years ago, but seeing the evidence of his bitterness and lack of trust, she knew she'd probably done more damage in leaving Nico than Kent's revelation would have. If only she could go back in time five years, to when they'd been blissfully happy. So many things she'd do differently. Her stomach sank and her knees buckled, but she wouldn't give in to the overwhelming regret while Nico was suffering.

She walked to within touching distance, wanting to reach out to him but knowing she was probably the last person he'd want comfort from now.

Instead of understanding how much she'd sacrificed so he'd never know, she'd become the enemy in his mind.

Nico turned to face the woman he could feel behind him. He still could tell where she was in a room without looking—a hyperawareness that had begun the first day they met picking grapes, side-by-side for the Jordan Wines harvest.

But he couldn't forget she was the woman who'd kept this secret from him. He gripped the frame of the swing set until his knuckles turned white. "Tell me your version of what my mother said."

Beth took a deep breath and held it for endless seconds. "After Kent came to my house and showed me the letters, he laid out the terms for his silence. I didn't know what to do, if the letters were even fake, but the risk to you if it were true and it got out... And Tim had suffered that major heart attack only months earlier—remember the doctors told us how important it was that he avoid stress?"

Nico felt the air in his lungs leave in a rush, but he forced them to refill. "We had plans for the next day. You couldn't have talked to me?"

Beth blinked several times in rapid succession then wrapped her arms around her waist. "Kent told me I had until midnight to make my decision or he was going to Tim. He said either way he was a winner."

Nico gripped the frame harder and swore.

"So I rang your mother and asked if she would see me. I told her it was about you, she agreed and drove over." Beth took a shuddering breath before continuing. "I asked her if you were Tim's son and waited for her to dismiss it—but she didn't. She begged me not to tell you."

He squared his shoulders. "Are you telling me that my mother was happy for you to be blackmailed into marriage?" He snorted his disbelief. "She knew what Kent was like and she loved you like a daughter. She'd never have agreed."

Beth shook her head. "I didn't tell her about Kent's conditions—she knew nothing of the blackmail. And soon after she was in the plane crash—" she paused and he knew she'd seen the flinch he'd been unable to hide, then she continued in a softer voice "—so I don't know if she worked it out before her death. But she told me all I needed to know."

Nico turned away, searching the sky that was no longer day though not yet night. A sky in limbo, like he'd been all these years.

Beth swallowed hard. "She pleaded with me not to tell you. She was desperate not to risk your happiness or Tim's health. With his heart condition, this shock could have literally killed him. But it was more even than that. She thought it would destroy you. She knew how close you were to Tim and how much you loved the winery. She couldn't bear for you to lose that…and neither could I," she ended on a whisper.

He whirled to face her, anger burning deep in his gut. "You think I would have preferred a false family than the woman I loved—and my real family, my son?" He thumped his chest with his fist and left it resting over his heart. Had she understood him at all?

"You were young, and first loves rarely last." She said the words almost in a chant, as if she'd repeated the same thing to herself regularly.

"Are you saying I would have left you? That if you hadn't deserted me…" His voice became thick and he stopped before he betrayed himself too far.

He would *never* have left her. Fool that he'd been, he'd believed their bond went too deep. Soul deep. Beyond love, beyond reason, beyond all else.

"You could fall in love again, but there were other things you could never get back—your father, your inheritance, your deep connection to the winery. They were irreplaceable."

Jagged pain tore into his heart. She really didn't know that he hadn't—couldn't—replace *her*. That there had been no serious woman in his life since. That the only woman he'd ever loved was this one who'd walked out on him without looking back, even while bearing his child.

"Would you have ever told me?" He cleared his throat before continuing. "Would you have kept Marco from me for our entire lives?"

"I promise you, I was going to tell you after your father passed away. Adelina had asked me not to risk his health with the stress of finding out, and I couldn't bear tainting your last days together by making you keep a secret from him."

He shook his head at her blindness to the right course of action. "Stress or not, he had a right to be told."

"Nico, please…" Beth's voice trailed off, but not before a tremor betrayed the distress she was clearly trying to mask.

His gaze roamed from her soulful sapphire blue eyes to her lush mouth. The word "please" brought back stark memories of her in his bed only hours before—of her begging him not to stop the sensual torment of her body. Of her taking him to the brink and him crashing over the other side. But they would never share a bed again. Not now he knew the truth.

"Thank you for your concern," he said coldly, "but it seems I didn't need to replace my father, my inheritance or the winery after all."

"I don't understand."

He held her gaze, unflinching. "I rang my father this afternoon. He needed to know, and he needed a chance to alter his will."

"What happened? What did he say?"

You're not my biological son, but don't you for a

second believe I'm not your father. I've raised you and I love you as much as any father could. You're mine.

Nico clenched his jaw and swallowed hard before answering. "He already knew. And he didn't change his will, so I'm not losing anything—the winery or my father."

You're my son, biology be damned. And there's no man on this Earth I'd rather have for a son. You make me proud every day.

"Nico, I'm sorry—" Her voice was soft, comforting, but he cut it off.

"You should have told me this story five years ago." His voice was tight as he struggled to control himself under the onslaught of the day. "Instead you made the decision for me. But it was *my* life and I should have been given the chance to sort it out myself. You didn't trust me to face the consequences, or live with them. You didn't know my father well enough to know he was sufficiently strong to handle the shock and that he'd still love me." He shook his head, disgusted by the whole mess. "The only good thing that's come out of this is that bastard Kent isn't my brother."

Her bottom lip trembled, her eyes were anguished. "I thought I was doing—"

"Yes, you *thought,* but it didn't matter what you thought. It was a secret about *me,* so it only mattered what *I* thought. Even if my father had disinherited me, it wouldn't matter—I have my own money. And my relationship with my father won't be hurt—neither will his heart."

She stumbled back but he followed, unwilling to give

her respite from a situation of her own making. She needed to hear how dearly her actions had cost him.

He dragged in a lungful of air, ensuring his voice didn't betray the pain inside him. "By delaying the inevitable, I've lost forever the chance to discuss it with my mother. And you've stolen four precious years with my son that I can never get back."

"Nico, I wish things could be different, that I'd made different choices five years ago, but you have to understand I was doing the best I could." Her hand snaked up to circle her throat. "I did it because I loved you."

The irony hit him squarely between the eyes. "You say you wish you'd made different choices? So you regret keeping the secret of my paternity from me, yet you did it all over again to Marco."

Beth's eyes were wide with grief as his dart hit its mark. For a suspended moment, his heart wanted to hold her and ease the pain she was also feeling. To take her inside and kiss her delectable mouth until her eyes lit with joy and desire instead. He almost reached for her.

Almost.

But, regardless of whether her motives were pure or not, he couldn't get past the knowledge that he'd never be able to trust her again.

So instead, he turned on his heel and walked out the door.

Eleven

Driving back to his hotel, Nico swerved the Alfa off the road and cut the engine. He'd finally ended things with the woman who'd betrayed him on so many levels, so why did he feel so damn wretched?

Blood pounding in his head, he got out and slammed the door. She'd hidden information about his own paternity from him and taken his son. Both crimes were unforgivable, but worse than these, *she'd left him alone for five years.*

He stalked into the moonlit vineyard, heart aching, remembering the nearly unbearable years without her. And yet, if she were to be believed, she'd been aching for him all this time, too....

He paused to run his hand along a strong sauvignon blanc vine. Would *he* have done any differently than

Beth five years ago? Wouldn't *he* have moved heaven and Earth to protect her, even if it meant losing her love and respect?

He swore and kicked the dirt with the toe of his shoe. Of course he would have. He'd have done more. And yet he'd never believed Beth capable of the same, or even questioned how things appeared.

He'd failed her.

Looking down the rows of bare vines, he saw his life stretch out before him, the joy of time with Marco the only bright spots in the emptiness and desolation that awaited him. And it was his own fault. His heart lurched in his chest. He'd held a slice of heaven in his hands and he'd squandered it.

All those years he'd blamed her. He'd believed Kent without question. Never believed in Beth. He never came for her or tried to see her. While she gave up everything for him and went through this alone, he'd played the field, trying in vain to convince himself he could be happy without her.

Beth had made mistakes, but they were mistakes committed because of love. She was still open, able to love without agenda, regardless of cost to herself—and an excellent mother, from the bond he'd seen between her and Marco.

And what had he done in the same time? Acquired money, possessions and a bitter heart. He thought of the wasted years they'd spent apart, the endless nights he'd ached for her. *Damn it, how could he have let this happen?*

Nothing could ever be more important than Beth

and their child. Frowning, he looked up at the crescent moon, above the vineyard. He'd already lost far too much time with them, with her—what in hell was he doing now out here, without her?

He strode back to the Alfa, gunned the engine and turned it around in a sharp 180, hoping it wasn't too late. That *he* wasn't too late.

Beth heard the knock on the door and tried to ignore it. Marco was at her parents', Nico would be at his hotel, and she couldn't entertain company right now—she could feel her face was blotchy, her eyes swollen. Nico had made it clear he'd never forgive her and she wasn't sure she could stand the pain. All she wanted to do was curl up and sleep in a darkened room for three days straight.

The knock came again, louder this time. Still she ignored it, gripping her sides with numb fingers. She couldn't blame him for not forgiving her—she only wished she'd apologized to him while she'd had the chance. After the way her decisions had hurt him, it was the very least she could do.

"Beth," a deep voice called through the door.

Her breath caught in her throat. *Nico*. She wiped her cheeks on her inside sleeve and pushed to her feet, her heart racing in anticipation of seeing him again.

No. She couldn't afford to get excited. He must have forgotten to tell her something to do with Marco, or needed other papers from Kent's things. That was fine, she'd let him say or do what he needed, but she'd take this second chance to apologize, too.

"Beth, I know you're home," Nico called.

"I'm coming." She checked herself in the hall mirror and confirmed her suspicions that she was a mess from crying, but she didn't have time to make any changes beyond wiping her face again and combing her fingers through her hair. She took a deep breath and opened the door to the father of her child for the second time in one evening. For the fourth time in one weekend.

The sight of him stole the air from her lungs. Even with the strain of the past two days showing around his dark brown eyes, he looked like a fallen angel— beautiful and dangerous.

She'd never loved him more, her chest *ached* with the weight of it.

But she pushed it down, back, away. Love meant little against the barriers that sat between them. Nico would never truly forgive her for keeping his son from him, or for not sharing the information about his biological father with him. And he was right not to forgive her. She'd thought at the time she was doing the best thing, but she'd give anything to go back in time and do things differently. Properly.

She blinked and collected herself. "Hello, Nico."

He didn't reply, seemed to be waiting. It wasn't till she met his eyes that he spoke. "Hello, Beth," he said, tension clear in his voice.

He opened his mouth to say more but she interrupted. "Before you tell me what you're here about, there's something I need to say."

He frowned but nodded. "All right."

Suddenly nervous, she stepped back. "Would you like to come inside?"

He nodded again before stamping his feet on the mat and following her in.

She paused at the arch leading to the kitchen. "Would you like something? A glass of wine?" She didn't expect him to accept, thinking he'd want to get out as soon as he could, so when he nodded once more, she was surprised. But she didn't question it—as long as he was here, she could say the words that needed to be said.

She poured them both a glass of pinot noir, passing him one and gestured to the chairs in front of the crackling fire. He sat on the edge of his seat with his forearms resting on his knees, looking down into the glass of rich red liquid. He looked as though he was working up to saying something as well, so she needed to get her apology out first. Before things became even more frosty between them.

She gripped the stem of her glass a little tighter, then met his eyes. "I know sorry will never be enough, but I want you to understand that I will never forgive myself for the decisions I've made."

"No, Beth, I—"

"Please." She laid an impulsive hand on his forearm, then retracted it when she realized the familiarity that gesture assumed. "Please let me say this. I need to."

His eyes flicked from her hand to his forearm where it had lain barely moments before. "Okay," he said slowly in a rasping voice.

"I hope one day we'll be able to have a polite relationship for Marco's sake, but if you can't bring yourself to do that, I'll respect your feelings. This situation is of my doing, and I accept that. It's—"

He placed a finger gently over her lips. "*Bella,* don't say another word." He removed the finger, almost reluctantly. "I've done worse things to you in the past five years than you're even capable of."

Beth frowned, trying to understand his meaning. "But you haven't done anything."

"Exactly. I did nothing." He scrubbed his fingers through his hair, suddenly seeming frustrated at himself. "I didn't find you and ask what had happened. If I hadn't believed what Kent told me, *if I'd come for you,* you wouldn't have had to live with him for five years."

She shook her head slowly. "But how could you know he was lying?"

"If I'd had faith in you," he said simply.

She closed her eyes for a long moment against the anguish that sentiment caused. She'd never expected he'd have that much faith in her—it was unrealistic for anyone to when they'd been abandoned the way she'd left him. But, oh, what a beautiful thought, knowing someone had that much faith in her....

Though, she'd been so determined—it would have made no difference. "Nico, even if you'd followed, I wouldn't have told you the truth."

"If I'd seen you with Kent, you wouldn't have been able to hide your feelings for him from me. I knew your expressions, your body language too well. As soon as I'd realized something was wrong, I wouldn't have given up until I knew the full story."

For one sweet moment, her mind followed the story

he wove with its alternate ending. But, reality was, she would have done anything in her power to keep the truth from him if he *had* followed.

She leaned a little closer to him over her armrest. "Nico, don't put yourself through this. You couldn't have known."

"I should have had faith," he said resolutely. "I made the wrong decision five years ago. It seems that you knew me better than I knew you back then."

She felt her jaw slacken as the implication of his words hit. "You think I did the right thing?"

"I still wish with everything inside me that you hadn't left that night." His eyes swam with emotion. "But I have to admit you were probably right—I would have handled the news even worse as a twenty-four-year-old than I did tonight." He smiled ruefully at her.

She sipped her wine and turned away from him, not sure how much more of this postmortem she could stand. She'd meant to simply apologize and hopefully create the foundation for a civilized relationship to allow for transfers of Marco at school holidays. But this…this was fast becoming intolerably painful.

She sucked in a breath and held it for seconds before speaking. "Is there any point talking about what would or wouldn't have happened? Surely it's better for everyone if we try to put it behind us."

"It's very relevant, my Beth," he said in a low, sure voice. "I had things the wrong way around."

"What do you mean?"

One corner of his sensual mouth slowly hitched in a half smile. "Did you know, if Kent hadn't taken you away, I'd have proposed—I'd been searching for the perfect ring for a month." He looked down into the glass of wine he'd barely touched, swirling it. "After you left, I tried to bury that memory, it hurt too much."

Tears for him pricked at the back of her eyes, but she held them at bay. "That was then."

He looked up, reached over and ran the back of his knuckles along her cheek. "I'm asking for your forgiveness. For your love."

Then he took a deep breath, lifted her free hand in his and met her gaze. "Beth, I love you. I want us to marry as we should have all those years ago."

She took a sip of wine before answering, using the pause to compose herself. Two proposals in one day, both from the man she loved, yet neither the one she yearned for. "If I agreed, I'd be deluding myself about what you really want."

His grip on her hand became more urgent. "And what is that?"

"You can see Marco as much as you want to, Nico." She released her hand from his and turned away to watch the crackling, sparking fire. "You don't have to marry me for that."

"I do want us to live together as a family, but this proposal isn't about Marco. And it's not the same as the thoughtless proposal I made this afternoon. I should never have asked you that way and I apologize," he said, his voice grim.

Beth looked back to him sitting so tall and strong in the fireside chair, but didn't dare to believe these were the words she'd heard so often in her dreams. She'd been building castles in the air for so many years, praying they'd one day have a future, that she knew she was in danger of projecting that very fantasy onto Nico's words now.

She squeezed her eyes shut in a long blink, trying to keep a clear mind. "I wish things could be that simple."

"They are." His expression changed, his eyes becoming fathomless with emotion.

Her heart skipped one beat then raced with the enormity of the possibilities. But she had to be certain. She inhaled a slow breath, giving herself time to form the words. "Tell, me, what sort of foundation do you think we have for a life together?"

Hope flickered in his eyes as he leaned over and reclaimed her hand, laying it against his chest. His eyes blazed with intent. "We have the best foundation for a life together, *bella*," he rasped. "Love. A love that has weathered every test that could possibly be thrown at it." He reached his free hand to tenderly smooth the hair from her face. "A love that never died or faded. And it's stronger now than ever."

She stared up at him, hardly daring to believe.

He turned her hand over and caressed a small circle on her palm. "I will always have trust and faith in you," he said. "I will have your back when things get tough."

What if it could be true? If he could still love her as he once had? Nico, the man she loved with every fiber of her being. Her heart fluttered wildly.

His eyes of deepest brown softened and the hand

that still held hers gripped tight. "I think I was always hoping we'd find our way back to our future one day. I know in my soul that our love is deeper than the oceans, can withstand anything, can last the test of time."

A wave of pure joy crashed over and through her, shining out from within her. "Oh, Nico," she said, though so many more words swam around her mind.

All she could do was accept his love, knowing it was untainted by the past and stronger than ever before.

He went to her, lifting her, and brought her back to sit in the cradle of his arms. Then, holding her tightly, he gently touched his mouth to hers. "You're the best part of me," he said against her lips.

She eased back, framing his face with her hands, wanting him to know this more than anything. "I've always loved you. Not a day went by since we've been apart, that I haven't thought of you and hoped this moment would come."

Nico's mouth curved wide in a smile, and yet it was more than that—his eyes smiled, his whole face. It was the smile he'd worn so often when they were younger, and her heart melted.

He lifted her out of his lap and knelt in front of her, then gently pulled her to kneel as well, mirroring him. Taking her hands again, he held them in the space between their bodies.

His eyes looked intensely into hers as if he could see her soul. "Now and forever," he whispered, "I pledge myself to you. No matter what's thrown our way, I'll never let anything come between us again."

Tears filled her eyes as she felt his vow to her very

core. "Now and forever, I pledge myself to you," she repeated. "For better or for worse, I will always be there for you."

He leaned in, pulling her flush against his body and kissed her again. Beth wrapped her arms around his neck, holding tight, intending never to let him go.

Epilogue

Three years later

"Hey, Dad!" Marco's voice was bright with enthusiasm. "What about this bunch?"

Beth stalled her secateurs at her own bunch and tilted her straw hat to watch Marco discuss the pinot noir grapes with his father in their private vineyard.

"They're ready." As he spoke, Nico absently caressed the hand of his sleeping eight-month-old daughter, snug in her sling against his chest. "Cut them off and add them to the cart."

Marco cut the grapes and deposited them in the cart with much flourish. "Grandpa Tim said when I go to Australia next, he's gonna show me how to work the destemmer."

Nico raised an eyebrow in mock surprise. "Grandpa Tim must think you're very good to let you destem the grapes at eight. He didn't let me touch the destemmer until I was twelve."

"He said I was the fastest learner he'd ever known," Marco said with pride.

Marco had grown so much through having a father who genuinely loved him and spent time with him. And the weekend sailing lessons Nico gave him on their new yacht out on the Sounds had allowed them to build the strong bond Beth had always wanted for Marco with his father. Nico's father Tim had improved and was feeling relatively healthy—he said it was thanks to Marco but Beth had wondered if having the secret about Nico's biology out in the open had played a small part in it, too.

"Dad, do you think this is a good bunch to take to Nanna? She said she wanted to see some I picked. She bought some other types of grapes at the shop and she's making me a pavlova and putting the eating grapes on top with cream since I'm being such a help with picking today."

"It's a perfect bunch to show Nanna." Nico smiled across at Beth in a moment of shared humor. Their son had turned into a chatterbox, giving constant commentaries on everyone and everything.

As their gazes held and locked, her husband's expression slowly changed, the amusement replaced by unguarded, profound love. Love for her. He'd looked at her this way before—often, in fact—but each time it still made the world stop spinning and her knees go weak.

He smiled, and she knew he felt the same.

Lizzie squirmed in her sling and yawned before she opened big brown eyes and blinked around at her family.

Beth put down her secateurs and took off her gloves, her heart overflowing at all her blessings. "Hey there, little Lizzie," she cooed before lifting her daughter free of the sling. "How was your sleep?"

Lizzie broke into a wide smile and waved her tiny fists in the air.

Beth looked at Nico under her lashes as she stage-whispered to her baby, "I always sleep best nestled against Daddy's chest, too."

Nico cast her a sizzling look that promised more than mere nestling after Marco and Lizzie were asleep, and her insides began a familiar slow burn. She'd never get enough of his hands touching her, of the intimacy they shared when completely alone.

Marco grabbed his sister's hand and kissed Lizzie on the cheek. "Can babies eat pavlova?"

"I think she might prefer her stewed apples for dessert." Beth grinned. Her mother was at home preparing a dinner for them all tonight to celebrate Nico being awarded New Zealand Winemaker of the Year. The meringue dessert she was making was actually for that dinner, too, but Beth knew her mother would have told Marco it was for him. Marco and Lizzie were the center of their grandparents' worlds.

A black flash raced between the rows of vines, then

Oliver appeared, dropping a stick at Marco's feet. He stepped back, intent eyes flicking between his playmate and the stick he'd found, willing Marco to get the message.

"Ollie, I can't play now," Marco said in overly dramatic exasperation. "I hafta pick grapes, see?" He held a bunch aloft in explanation.

Oliver's soft, black forehead wrinkled, pulling his ears higher as he tried to understand.

Nico's shoulders shook with suppressed laughter, but he couldn't hold it back and coughed several times to cover. He took Marco's basket from his hands. "You can go and play. You've done a lot here already and your mum and I can finish off."

"Cool!" Marco ripped off his gloves, picked up the stick and threw it as far as he could. Then he and Oliver took off after it.

After he watched them leave, Nico leaned in and kissed Beth tenderly on the mouth. The pure love contained in the one simple kiss sang through her veins. "Do you know, it's nine years ago this harvest that I saw a gorgeous creature with strawberry blond hair piled up under her hat picking grapes at my family's winery."

Her mind raced back to that day, to the feeling of being swept away by a stranger's glance. She'd never felt anything as powerful before, but it was nothing to the depths their love had grown into. Their time apart, the mountains they'd overcome, had only made their love more solid, more precious.

She laid a palm lovingly against the side of his face. "That's a coincidence," she whispered past a lump in her throat, "because it was almost nine years ago at a harvest that I first saw a tall, broad man with eyes I fell into. And I still haven't resurfaced."

He leaned over Lizzie, embracing both his wife and daughter and kissed Beth in a long, soft kiss that promised her all she could ever want.

*Rancher Ramsey Westmoreland's temporary cook
is way too attractive for his liking.
Little does he know Chloe Burton came to his ranch
with another agenda entirely....*

That man across the street had to be, without a doubt, the most handsome man she'd ever seen.

Chloe Burton's pulse beat rhythmically as he stopped to talk to another man in front of a feed store. He was tall, dark and every inch of sexy—from his Stetson to the well-worn leather boots on his feet. And from the way his jeans and Western shirt fit his broad muscular shoulders, it was quite obvious he had everything it took to separate the men from the boys. The combination was enough to corrupt any woman's mind and had her weakening even from a distance. Her body felt flushed. It was hot. Unsettled.

Over the past year the only male who had gotten her time and attention had been the e-mail. That was simply pathetic, especially since now she was practically drooling simply at the sight of a man. Even his stance—both hands in his jeans pockets, legs braced apart, was a pose she would carry to her dreams.

And he was smiling, evidently enjoying the conversation being exchanged. He had dimples, incredibly sexy dimples in not one but both cheeks.

"What are you staring at, Clo?"

Chloe nearly jumped. She'd forgotten she had a lunch date. She glanced over the table at her best friend from college, Lucia Conyers.

"Take a look at that man across the street in the blue shirt, Lucia. Will he not be perfect for Denver's first issue of *Simply Irresistible* or what?" Chloe asked with so much excitement she almost couldn't stand it.

She was the owner of *Simply Irresistible*, a magazine for today's up-and-coming woman. Their once-a-year Irresistible Man cover, which highlighted a man the magazine felt deserved the honor, had increased sales enough for Chloe to open a Denver office.

When Lucia didn't say anything but kept staring, Chloe's smile widened. "Well?"

Lucia glanced across the booth at her. "Since you asked, I'll tell you what I see. One of the Westmorelands—Ramsey Westmoreland. And yes, he'd be perfect for the cover, but he won't do it."

Chloe raised a brow. "He'd get paid for his services, of course."

Lucia laughed and shook her head. "Getting paid won't be the issue, Clo—Ramsey is one of the wealthiest sheep ranchers in this part of Colorado. But everyone knows what a private person he is. Trust me—he won't do it."

Chloe couldn't help but smile. The man was the epitome of what she was looking for in a magazine cover and she was determined that whatever it took, he would be it.

"Umm, I don't like that look on your face, Chloe. I've seen it before and know exactly what it means."

She watched as Ramsey Westmoreland entered the store with a swagger that made her almost breathless. She *would* be seeing him again.

Look for Silhouette Desire's
HOT WESTMORELAND NIGHTS
by Brenda Jackson,
available March 9 wherever books are sold.

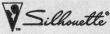

REQUEST YOUR FREE BOOKS!

**2 FREE NOVELS
PLUS 2
FREE GIFTS!**

Passionate, Powerful, Provocative!

YES! Please send me 2 FREE Silhouette Desire® novels and my 2 FREE gifts (gifts are worth about $10). After receiving them, if I don't wish to receive any more books, I can return the shipping statement marked "cancel." If I don't cancel, I will receive 6 brand-new novels every month and be billed just $4.05 per book in the U.S. or $4.74 per book in Canada. That's a saving of almost 15% off the cover price! It's quite a bargain! Shipping and handling is just 50¢ per book in the U.S. and 75¢ per book in Canada.* I understand that accepting the 2 free books and gifts places me under no obligation to buy anything. I can always return a shipment and cancel at any time. Even if I never buy another book, the two free books and gifts are mine to keep forever.

225 SDN E39X 326 SDN E4AA

Name _____ (PLEASE PRINT) _____

Address _____ Apt. # _____

City _____ State/Prov. _____ Zip/Postal Code _____

Signature (if under 18, a parent or guardian must sign)

Mail to the **Silhouette Reader Service**:
IN U.S.A.: P.O. Box 1867, Buffalo, NY 14240-1867
IN CANADA: P.O. Box 609, Fort Erie, Ontario L2A 5X3

Not valid for current subscribers to Silhouette Desire books.

Want to try two free books from another line?
Call 1-800-873-8635 or visit www.morefreebooks.com.

* Terms and prices subject to change without notice. Prices do not include applicable taxes. N.Y. residents add applicable sales tax. Canadian residents will be charged applicable provincial taxes and GST. Offer not valid in Quebec. This offer is limited to one order per household. All orders subject to approval. Credit or debit balances in a customer's account(s) may be offset by any other outstanding balance owed by or to the customer. Please allow 4 to 6 weeks for delivery. Offer available while quantities last.

Your Privacy: Silhouette Books is committed to protecting your privacy. Our Privacy Policy is available online at www.eHarlequin.com or upon request from the Reader Service. From time to time we make our lists of customers available to reputable third parties who may have a product or service of interest to you. If you would prefer we not share your name and address, please check here. ☐

Help us get it right—We strive for accurate, respectful and relevant communications. To clarify or modify your communication preferences, visit us at www.ReaderService.com/consumerschoice.

SDES10

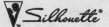

SPECIAL EDITION

FROM *USA TODAY* BESTSELLING AUTHOR

CHRISTINE RIMMER

BRAVO FAMILY TIES

A BRIDE FOR JERICHO BRAVO

Marnie Jones had long ago buried her wild-child
impulses and opted to be "safe," romantically
speaking. But one look at born rebel Jericho Bravo
and she began to wonder if her thrill-seeking side
was about to be revived. Because if ever there was
a man worth taking a chance on, there he was,
right within her grasp....

*Available in March
wherever books are sold.*